MW00774659

SKKYPTOR

Luminous Volumes

ALR019

Published by

Aqualamb

SKRYPTOR:
Tim Garrigan: Guitars
David McClelland: Bass VI
Hank Shteamer: Drums

ALBUM CREDITS:
Recorded and mixed by Colin Marston at Menegroth,
the Thousand Caves, March 2018
Mastered by Carl Saff

Tim Garrigan: keyboards, #s 1, 2, 3 and 6
Colin Marston: Mellotron, # 7
David McClelland: keyboards, #s 2, 3 and 6. Xtra gtr, #s 4,5 and 7.

Cover art: David McClelland
Illustration assistance: Stephany Sovitch
Album design: Aqualamb

All Songs written by SKRYPTOR

BOOK CREDITS
First Printing: Edition of 500
ISBN: 978-0-9985211-5-2

David McClelland - Story Curation
Joy Sanchez - Copy Editor
Charlie Curnow - Copy Editor

skryptor.bandcamp.com
aqualamb.org
sleepinggiantglossolalia.bandcamp.com
skingraft.com

Master of Ceremonies
by Sean Madigan Hoen – Illustration by David McClelland 1

Dry Cleaning
by David McClelland – Illustration by Fritz Welch 31

The Sound of the Bridge
by Tom Newton – Illustration by Sarah Austensen Wilson 43

Memories
by William A. Turley – Illustration by Guno Park 59

Brendan Ryan's Rocket Car
by David McClelland – Illustration by Jimi Sakai 79

Brights
by Chaunceton Bird – Illustration by Rich Hall 105

Slaughterhouse Vision
by Maria Gabriele Baker – Illustration by Paul Nitsche 120

Stork
by Jeremy Johnston – Illustration by Rich Hall 133

For Your Kindness, For Your
Buttons by Ian Caskey – Illustration by Stephany Sovitch 151

Brothers
by David McClelland – Illustration by Jenna Cha 169

Surfin' Turf
by Sarah Blank – Illustration by The Hopeless Artist 191

God of Thunder
by Sean Madigan Hoen – Illustration by Nate Hillyer 217

Asylum
by Benjamin Smart – Illustration by Millie Benson 227

The music for *Luminous Volumes*
can be downloaded via the link below:

aqualamb.org/019

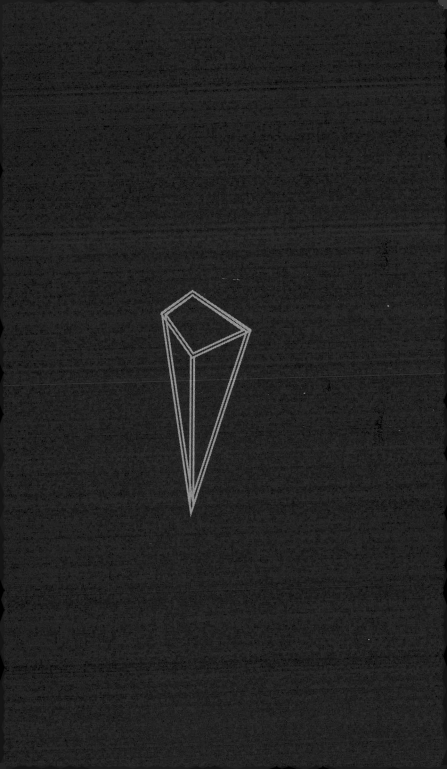

David McClelland

SEAN MADIGAN HOEN

Master of Ceremonies

John was back in the country two days when, amid a concussive headache and a dirty, full-body itch, he draped himself over the toilet and upchucked silver bile for the better part of a morning. His abdominals clenched so tightly they were hot to the touch and his mess began to pinken with traces of blood. The nastiest case of jet jag in the annals of international travel, John figured, in a daze, just before he lost consciousness. His final vision before the fever pulled him under was of a barefooted child pitching forth a dirt-colored tennis ball that would not meet his opened hands. He lay facedown and sweating on the tiles until his sister Lisa came upon him with a scream so gory it drew open one of his eyes. By nightfall, Henry Ford Hospital had begun draining every ounce of hemoglobin from his veins to refill him with bag after bag of someone else's Type O Positive.

"If you hadn't come back in time..." were the first words John heard upon waking a day later. Lisa hunched over him, fingering crust from his eyes and tidying the brown strands that had escaped his ponytail. "Who woulda found you," she said, "if you hadn't come home?"

The doctors kept him for seven days in the ICU, analyzing his functions and nourishing him through tubes. Never failing to note what a merciful coincidence it was that he'd returned to Detroit before the parasites—several different species, apparently; one categorized as malaria—began waging their ravages. If only with a nod, John conceded the risks of African blood banks, imagining how far gone he might have been before someone carted him to Abidjan, the city nearest the village where he'd stationed himself somewhat beyond the bounds of the Peace Corps' advisement. Discharged from the hospital, he understood the episode to be his body's way of admitting it was now, after a period of exertion, safe to heal and purge. His eyes were creek-water gray and his vision had yet to regain its eagle-eyed clarity. He knew from having checked that his penis was shrunken, clammy to the touch. Recovery would take weeks, but at last he'd settled into to his Southeast Detroit apartment, the place he'd most longed for during his twenty-four months abroad.

He had a three-cushion sofa, a stack of books on urban farming, a television and an old VHS deck. A Schwinn ten-speed hung from hooks—even chained to a fence it would've stood no chance in the neighborhood below. On a coffee table were a set of djembe drums and the dusty tennis ball he'd clutched during his fourteen-hour flight home. John had a thousand memories of the Ivory Coast, the best being the village boys he'd tossed the ball with every morning and the worst being a dog he'd bludgeoned with a stone.

He'd yet to speak of the dog or the trenches he'd dug in African soil, the miles of PVC piping he'd laid: Low-cost drip systems. Lisa was on red alert; mention of his endeavors would cause further duress. During lunch breaks, she'd been stopping by with frozen meals and VHS tapes. Monday was Blade Runner; Tuesday, The Running Man—sufferable movies John played when his kidneys ached. Otherwise he lay on the sofa, tangling with the fact he'd come close to death or permanent damage while theorizing what it could mean for his homecoming. The doctors had ordered a month of leisure. Pneumonia was a risk. The antibiotics taxed his intestines. His mouth tasted of yeast. He'd never have known his time convalescing was coinciding with a killer on the loose had Lisa not come by for a Wednesday visit with two slices of pizza and an expression like she'd witnessed the death of Christ.

"A psychopath," she said, jerking her thumb toward the street-side window. "Right over there, few blocks west of Vernor."

Above a vacated flower shop on Griggs and Grand River— the edge of a forlorn hood—John's one-bedroom was such a hard sell that his landlady had agreed to a measly lump sum, the price of a storage unit, allowing him to keep the lease while abroad. "What psychopath?" he said. "Is this the latest scheme to suburbanize me? You can't give it a week?"

"It's not about you," Lisa said, daubing pizza grease with a napkin.

She lived in Garden City, the drab burb they'd been raised in, fifteen miles west of city limits. Few white folk had remained in Detroit proper by the time they'd been born in the early '80s. Their mom had long ago moved upstate, where she'd passed on as peacefully as one could hope. To the Africans, John had identified as a Detroiter, tried and true. They'd known Motown, Eminem and Cadillac.

"You read the news?" said Lisa.

Their tastes had always differed: his on the cultural and political fringes; hers fantastical and pop. His tube television lacked a type of digital converter you needed to catch a signal these days. He'd yet to have internet reinstalled.

"So, what happened?" he said. "Someone get shot?"

"I wish they got shot."

She wore her dental assistant getup: slacks and a blouse, the sleeves rolled, smears of aqua paste. She'd let her frizzed blonde hair have its way, sprouting wild and coily, practically exotic for Wayne County. John was glad to see it. She'd also managed to keep the midwestern thirtysomething bulk off her thighs and midriff. John was thirty-three, Lisa's junior by two years. She held the grease-slicked napkin like a post-op towelette but had yet to taste her pizza. With little appetite, John took a nibble.

"Bet that tastes good," she said. "When's the last time you had a real slice?"

"I haven't heard murder reports in a while"

"I mean, this is a serious whack job," she said. "He did a house of three guys, chopped them up afterward and everything."

"Whoa."

"Right over there." She nodded toward the window. "In your freakin' backyard, just about."

"Drug related?"

"News is saying the victims were some shady characters, but the killer walks in like nothing, hacks 'em up and then goes and paints their front door in blood. Wrote some creepy devil stuff."

"Devil stuff?" Pizza tang stung John's chapped lips. Every word spoken was an expenditure. He breathed deep and mustered the next. "You could get away with just about anything over there. East of Vernor, anyway."

Lisa said, "You go all the way around the world and come back to live in hell."

If anything, installing irrigation systems in those impoverished villages had vitalized John to return and be of use on home turf. He'd learned to draft blueprints and work in phases, had plans to renovate the overgrown public park on Charleston Street. Detroit's business district had begun to thrive on tax-payer–funded endeavors, yet the city at large, this giant slab of geography—the real people—remained largely desolated. "It's some crack addict," he said. "Had a fight with his dealers and went mental."

"Remember those satanic rappers?" Lisa asked. "That's what this reminds me of. Goons flashing devil horns, airbrushing pentagrams onto the hoods of their cars."

"Yeah, okay."

It'd been a D-town fad for a hot minute during the early '90s: Local rappers named Esham and Natas and Jah-Lucifari rhyming about being in cahoots with the Prince of Darkness. Stringing up corpses. Boomin' words from hell. Verse upon verse of necromantic wordplay. Forget corny movies, John's adolescent inspirations had been the bass-heavy sounds of the city. Back in Garden City, he'd dressed in Esham's baggy-panted street-Diablo style. He'd hoarded cassettes and memorized lyrics, and it wasn't until he discovered Fela Kuti's prophetic jams that he disavowed the insidiousness of such counterproductive themes.

"Six-six-six," rapped John, weak in the voice, "The crucifix/ Hell was the fire on the candlesticks."

"Heck is that?"

"Esham—the evil M.C."

"Gawd," said Lisa.

The performance left him winded. He abandoned his slice. Why on earth she thought his bowels could manage a slab of processed mozzarella and starch, he couldn't fathom—carrot juice, live enzymes were what he needed.

"You come stay at my place?" she said. "I'll pick you up after work."

"I'm home—I'll dim my soul with whatever movie you brought and then I'll sleep fourteen hours. Tomorrow, I'm a new man."

"Don't push it, evil M.C. For once in your life."

With his right hand John threw up a sign, his fingers contorting until they replicated "The Hatchet Man," devil-rap street code for Your End iz Near.

When the sunlight went orange and dusty, John lugged himself to the bathroom for his first proper shower since the hospital. Enough of the dead-skin flakes. The sharp, glandular groin odor. He tugged down his sweatpants and observed himself. Several pounds had been lost. Faint tan lines remained where his cut-off jeans had let his thighs be bronzed by African sun. His legs were faded rickets, a putty of keloid scar tissue on the left calf.

For two years he'd rinsed mostly beneath jimmied hoses

sputtering cold drips. Now the soft city water, its full-tilt pressure, made noodles of his limbs. He scrubbed as long as he could before turning off the spigot to sit in the tub. He leaned his head back against the tiles, one numbing leg dangled over the enameled lip. Closing his eyes, he saw the dog, the rock cracking its eye socket. After having slept a few nights at his side, the stray—a shepherd with strange gold markings—turned violent and bared its fangs. Burying the creature, staring down at its zags of yellow fur, John named it Laser. Afterward a green-eyed Californian named Heidi led him into her tent to sterilize his gnashed leg and knead his shoulders as he wept. They were near in age, two Americans on a primarily Australian crew, and for months he'd tried to remain impartial to her sunblasted face, the freckles multiplying on her clavicle. By the end of their tenure, before he'd gone maverick, Heidi had developed a tic of clasping his ponytail as they spooned on her cot. John would wriggle free and, in her sleep, she'd grasp again for his tuft. She'd be doing that now. She'd slide into the tub and tuck herself beside him, taking hold of his brown rein...

A knock downstairs, echoing up the stairwell.

John cracked an eye. The bathroom had gone dark and his fingers were pruned.

Three more knocks.

"Hey, all right," he said.

With any luck it was the landlady, whom he'd written to about turning the unrentable storefront below into a co-op where people might consign local produce and gather for communal happenings. The old loon was on a schedule where John had met her twice in six years. Wrapping a towel around his waist, he dragged a half-asleep leg down the stairs, to the entrance, the window of which was shuttered with sheet metal. Sliding the deadbolt, he cracked the door. Outside was summertime darkness, the pavement lit by the avenue's scant streetlights. He stuck his head into the night and caught the rumps of two young women strutting down Woodward.

"Hey," he said.

The girls turned to gaze at his face where it hovered along the doorframe.

"Were you knocking?" he said.

They moved toward him, one carrying a manila folder and the other with eyes that meant business. "You decent?" said the caustic one, about sixteen, with runty dreadlocks and skintight shorts they'd called "painted on" back in Garden City.

"I was in the shower." He'd yet to fasten his ponytail. The wet thatch hung down near his nipples. With a twitch of his neck he tossed it back, securing the towel with both hands.

"You gonna put some clothes on?"

"I can't go up there and come back down again. I'm just outta the hospital."

"Well," said the girl. Her arms were sleek, dark and taut, her T-shirt sleeves cropped high. Scrappy. Many neighborhood girls appeared so. John figured the meaner they posed, the better.

"I thought you were the landlady," he said.

"And what's she do?"

"She's half crazy."

The girls looked the avenue up and down.

"We're organizing a neighborhood watch," said the one doing the talking. Her friend was dressed about the same, yet her face betrayed that she was the softy here. In a gentle trance, the quiet girl produced a flyer and offered it to John. The back of his head felt melon-like where it had pressed against the tile, the skin there pulsing as he fussed with his towel, freeing a hand.

"Uh-huh." He glanced the photocopy: a crude sketch of white man wearing a sock hat, broad strokes forming the shoulders. "Who's that?" he said.

"That's the pyscho's been wasting people," said the girl.

"They saw him?"

"She right here saw him." The girl nodded toward her friend, who appeared stunned, with a face John found difficult to linger on. "Saw him scoping the scene of the crime, day before it happened."

"Man-oh-man," he said. "Is this an official sketch?"

Cars moved along Grand River, alighting the sidewalk.

"Police ain't doing nothing," said the girl. "And this ain't the first."

"What do you mean?"

"Couple guys on Oakland Street got cut up two weeks ago."

"Were they dealers, too?"

"What's that supposed to mean?" said the girl.

"I heard the guys who got killed were into drugs," John said.

The flyer had wilted, the image translucent and changing face.

"You think cause somebody's got their hands in something gives some maniac the right to terrorize our neighborhood, start hacking people?"

"No," said John. "No, no." His tongue was parched. Though the night was warm, a chill started through his legs, rising from the crumbled tile of the vestibule. It wasn't that he wondered where the new blood in his veins had come from so much as what his organs were making of it. He should've eaten the pizza; low-sugar tremors were giving him an out-of-body scare.

"I was in the Peace Corps," he said.

"You a Marine?" said the girl. "Look like a junkie, not no Marine."

"I was in Africa doing irrigation work, trying to address the running water situation."

"Look like you crawled up from a graveyard."

"I was real sick."

"Africa," she told her silent friend. "Guy says he's been in Africa."

"I almost died."

"Bet you did," she said. "You just keep an eye out for your killer friend out there all wasting people."

They pivoted and began tromping up the block.

"Hey," John said. "I wanna join the watch."

"Yeah?" The girl turned, extending her finger straight at him. "Then you just did."

After a few days of medicine and Lisa's VHS tapes, all the while squeezing his tennis ball, John was feeling spry enough to collect the mail and shower each afternoon. Over the weekend he'd watched a crap flick called Vision Quest twice because it featured a scene in which the protagonist trains obsessively for a wrestling match. It inspired recuperation. When Lisa came by that Monday, he dropped and did seven push-ups.

"Bodies," he said. "Amazing machines. You're on the verge

of death and then you're right back in action."

"Brother," Lisa said, making for his fridge to take stock of the frozen dinners she'd stowed. "You gotta eat."

"Get me some greens. I need superfoods, earth stuff. The soil is so rich on the coast, you wouldn't believe the colors..."

"I got the Lean Cuisine. How's this one: 'Mandarin chicken with steamed vegetables on a bed of luscious rice,' it says."

"That's from a laboratory."

Lisa swung shut the freezer door, plucking the flyer from beneath a Peace Corps magnet. "What's this?"

"That's the nutcase who whacked those guys a few streets over."

"Bull," she said. "They don't have any leads."

"How do you know?"

"Cause he did it again over the weekend. Walked in and kills two more guys. About half a minute down the road from here."

"Stop it."

"Serious," she said. "Another drug house. Papers said the freak musta been in there for hours. Then he walks out as the sun's coming up and nobody sees a thing, not even him doodling blood on the door, just like he did in the other place."

"And you're just now telling me?"

"'Cause what do you do? You start rapping like the evil M.C. Seems like he's killing criminals, anyway. He's not coming for you, veggie man." Lisa flipped him the bird. "Where'd you get this flyer?" she said. "Looks like a three-year-old drew it."

"Girl in the neighborhood. She saw him."

"The Grand River Reaper."

"You're kidding?"

"That's what they're calling him. People are hysterical. How about you check the news so you know whether or not to walk outside. There were all these people walking the streets the other night, rallying with bats and pipes like it's Mad Max shit."

"Mad Max." The reference took him a minute.

"And the cops didn't do a thing, just let Channel Four film everybody, these hoodlums, talking like they're defending their turf."

"Once the media gets a hold of it—" said John. He walked to the window and gazed onto Grand River. A fine day, nothing amiss but a few shopping carts upturned on the sidewalk.

"Better be careful," Lisa said, studying the flyer. "If they're thinking it's a white boy."

"Don't spin it that way. It's a psychopath, straight up."

"Well, I'm just saying, he's murdering these small-time crack dealers. It doesn't even make sense."

"Well, I'm saying, there's families around here. People getting by like anywhere else."

"You get yourself practically killed in the bush and now you're here acting like you're part of some community."

"I wasn't in the bush. I was on the coast, and now I'm on the neighborhood watch."

"You get him, then," Lisa said. "Catch the guy while he's spilling blood in some crack house."

"Half the problem is your attitude."

He couldn't tell if she wore the same outfit to work every day or if she had a week's worth of identical blouses, but her eyes were misting. She dug her nails into her blond coils, hissing the way she would before a long cry.

"Okay, now," he said. "We're just talking."

"I've gotta get to work," she said. "I brought more tapes. They're in that bag with the food you won't eat."

"You bring Mad Max?"

"Fuck's sake," she said, waving him from sight.

John set one of the Lean Cuisines in the oven and nuked it on max. Its eggplant fettuccini appeared pre-bathed in a gelatinous sludge but, like everything else, the entree didn't taste like much. A flick called The Golden Child played on the VCR. As with the other movies, John realized Lisa had been quoting it for years—It's your destiny to seek some serious psychiatric help—turns of phrase he'd believed to be her own inventions.

Around dusk, he walked down to the avenue. He stood gazing east, volleying the tennis ball with the concrete. Grand River led to the heart of Detroit, where it tangled with Michigan Avenue in the district that began rejuvenating after the 2005 Super Bowl came to town and Dan Gilbert, a right-wing mortgage entrepreneur, began huge developments. En route to the gentrified locus there were mansions, boarded up and graffitied—elegant three-story homes with circular drives and gilded stone and Victorian masonry, in wait since the '70s for white people to move back and reclaim them.

Turning out from a side street, two boys came skulking up Grand Ave. John had seen them before but they'd since grown inches. They wore matching red and black flannels. He caught the tennis ball off a bounce. With a lot of these young men, John understood it was imprudent to make yourself known. The villagers had laughed when he'd gotten shit-faced on Amarula and strutted his honkey moves, but Grand was a humorless strip. John's block conveyed a particular meanness, barren in a way that made you feel you had to contend with every oncoming shape. The boys moved slowly, shoulders broad, not taking John in so much as refusing to acknowledge him as a vital presence.

Only once had John been mugged, for twelve bucks, on his way out of Sunshine Grocery. The lone kid, wielding a knife, had all but thanked him after he'd handed over the money. But assaults were prevalent and murder occasional; there was no being cavalier. Playing it smooth was key, remaining conscious of the desperate straits flowing beneath the city. Before he'd left, Michigan's unemployment had cleared twenty percent and Detroit's population had dwindled to numbers not seen since the 1910s. The monthly stipend the Corps paid out was steady money he might not have otherwise seen. Heidi had listened to his city stories as if being read bedtime thrillers, yanking his ponytail to convey she'd never imagined such things back in Pasadena. "I was worried about coming here," she'd said of the impoverished shores of the Gulf of Guinea, "but you can talk to the people. They want to talk." And he'd told her, "I feel safer here, actually."

What made a difference, he'd concluded, was one human being talking to another, one at a time.

"'Scuse me," John said as the young men neared.

They kept their stride. "Yeah, what?" said one of them.

"You know two girls? Walking 'round here with flyers?"

The taller of the boys halted, alerting the other to shuffle backward a few paces before planting his feet. They posed in staggered formation, each with a bored, agitated look. "Flyers of what?" said the tall kid—sixteen, seventeen, flannel buttoned to the neck on a summer evening.

"Picture of the guy who's all wasting people." The words had the chunky street-beat of some lyric John wasn't meant to recite, like there was a whole system of gestures and hand smacks he might have studied before nerving up.

"Maybe I do." The kid leveled his chin. His shape slackened, settling into an ineffectual cock, defensive cool. Both boys drew interrogative faces, as if suspecting John of operating on the killer's behalf.

"Two girls said they were starting up a neighborhood watch," John said. "I'm looking to get involved if anyone needs help."

"Got all the help I need right here." The kid lifted the low-hanging hem of his flannel above his waist, where a pistol was tucked into his boxer shorts.

"All right," John said.

"So the motherfucker wants to step, let him step."

The kid's friend clucked, sagged deeper into his pose.

"Just looking to help," John said.

"You wanna know them girls?" said the kid, standing arms crossed. "Mr. Ponytail wants to know?"

"They gave me a flyer."

"They some tight ass bitches—but I show you where they live."

"Or just tell 'em to stop by again."

"Yeah? You want them stopping by?"

"You know, if there's any developments with the watch."

"You come on right now," said the kid. "I show you their house."

Had he felt strong, in possession of his wiles, John would

have taken the offer. It was a dare; also, perhaps, a rite of passage, on the other side of which his lack of fear might prove to these boys that he wasn't pegging them one way or the other. But he was afraid, as worried about his tired limbs as he was this gun-toter's potential to get stupid.

"Can't now," he said. "I have a friend coming over."

The kid smiled. "Girl with the blonde 'fro stopping by? That right?"

The thought of Lisa's hair having anything to do with anything put John into a hectic mood. Cool sweat beaded beneath his nostrils.

"She in and out," the kid laughed, nodding a yes-I-like-them-motherfuckin'-apples gesture toward his friend, who said, "Fo' sure, fo' sure."

"That's my sister," John said.

"A'right," said the kid, raising his hand for a smack.

"If you feel like telling those girls I'm around," John said, jutting forth his palm as the kid followed through with a lazy swipe. Their skin touched quickly.

"They live right over there. Way down the block. House with all the yellow shit on the porch. You'll see."

"Yellow shit?"

The kid fanned out his fingers and, as if flicking John from memory, waved backhanded, he and his friend turning on the heels of their sneakers to pace up the avenue.

The next morning John rang Lisa at work, demanding she phone him when she was on her way. Around noon she called back and rapped, "En route ta' Mister Evil M.C./ETA ten minutes away," bending the last syllable until it nearly rhymed.

John made for the street. The stairs were getting easier. He stood before the flower shop, eyeing traffic. Sun banged down, glinting off smashed bottles. When Lisa pulled her Ford Fiesta to the curb, John watched her dig a week's worth of The Detroit News from the backseat.

"You've got some research," she said, hefting the load. "Couldn't find my Mad Max tape, though. You'll have to go digital if you want the experience."

John scanned the avenue, wondering if those kids were tracking his visitors, or if they simply wandered around so often that they saw most of what went down.

"Let's go up," he said.

"And deprive ourselves of this wondrous view?"

"Lemme carry those."

Lisa's hair was raked into a plastic headband. A pretty woman, especially upon unveiling her supple face, the magenta skin tag above her left eye. John worried she loved him so fiercely she'd never settle on another man; he'd left the country hoping she'd be thrust into a new life, that there was a kind, cornball film buff awaiting her. "I got 'em," she said, cradling the papers. "You get the soup."

Upstairs, he didn't bother with the tomato broth. As Lisa peeled the lid off her Styrofoam container, he rifled through the metro sections, the police briefs.

"He says he wants soup and then he won't look at it," she said.

To symbolize his progress, he'd donned his cut-off jeans. Seated on the couch, his legs felt thin within the frayed denim.

"You feeling faint?"

"This thing's got me worked up," he said.

17

"They mentioned some unsolved deaths in Inkster. The guy is serial. It's like our own Jason Vorhees—you know, Friday the Thirteenth?"

"How do they figure it's one guy?"

"It's all in there somewhere," Lisa said. "How about you get a proper TV?"

"What's the TV say?"

"The cops or whoever suspect it's a lone dude. You know, they keep the evidence to themselves. The girls at work think maybe it's some religious sort of thing."

"Smearing blood on the door."

"I don't know," she said. "Maybe he isn't promoting evil but saying, like, 'Here lies the devil.'"

John's nerves had reanimated the hyperactivity of his left leg. It'd settled down overseas; now it was jittering again, always the left one.

"Will you eat your soup?" Lisa said. "And I was thinking—they've got an opening for a receptionist at the office and maybe you wanna check it out?"

John snorted.

"Oh, you're too good for that? A job's a job around here, 'case you haven't heard."

"I'm not too good for anything. But I'm not about to come out of what I've gone through and settle for mindless drudgery."

"So, what I do is mindless?"

"I didn't say that."

"Keeping people's teeth from rotting isn't important, but planting a garden in the hood is? Who's gonna buy your carrots down here?"

"Does it bother you so much that I believe in something?"

It'd been awhile since he'd spoken like this. He'd thought his work with the Corps would negate criticism of his ideals, that he'd never again be put to task for what Lisa used to call his "lower-middle-class guilt."

"What do you believe?" she said. "You leave for two years and come back half-dead. You ever think what that's like for someone who gives a shit?"

"I get it."

"Haven't had a girlfriend in seven years."

"I had one in the Corps," John said. "Heidi."

"Heidi," she said. "First I've heard."

"Where's the stuff about the killer?" John turned the pages. "I'm not seeing it."

Lisa lipped a spoonful of broth and scowled. A hollow blast came from the street. John leapt up, knocking over his soup to scramble for the window.

"Christ," Lisa said.

A rust bucket van slogged across Grand Ave. Before escaping view, its exhaust backfired again with a gust of dark smoke that John made out by squinting.

"I'm sorry," he said, keeled at the sill. "I'm losing my cool."

"You've been halfway around the world and caught malaria."

He wasn't as hardy as he'd thought. His chest quaked as he sat down. With no further warning than a tremble of his leg, he lapsed into a snotty cry as he began dabbing the puddled soup with newspaper.

"I'll get it," Lisa said, digging her hands into his shoulders as if to wring loose the tears. "Just go easy."

A splash of red broth had colored his kneecap, the fray of his shorts.

"There was this dog. I named him Laser."

"You had a pet, too," she said. "All kinds of friends over there."

The outburst left John feeling he'd regressed by degrees. His eyes bleared as he escorted his sister to the street. When they reached her Fiesta, Lisa hugged him around the neck. "Give yourself a break," she said as he laid his head against her collarbone. From that vantage he saw the boys, red clad and joined by a few others, loitering across Grand, not exactly looking his way but watching just the same. It was too late to be stealthy, to make it appear anything other than it was: John and the frizzy blonde girl. He shut his eyes and breathed into Lisa's blouse, the two of them standing in the open as the midday sun made things clear.

Much of the newsprint was smudged beyond legibility, yet the gist of the story was there. These killings were methodical. The articles were paradoxical and vague but agreed the perpetrator had done his victims with a bladed weapon. Despite the firearms reportedly found at both scenes, the killer had crept in and commenced his slashing without a single bullet being discharged. Evidently his knife work was a thing of calculation: not a stab more than necessary. The chief of police wasn't saying much beyond that the department was on the case and that the neighborhood in question was rough going. One article succumbed to portraying the crimes as Manson-like, while another interviewed neighbors who claimed they weren't surprised about what happened, so much as the nature of it. As for the blood-paintings on the porches, no theories had arisen.

As John read, the slight return of a feverish chill worked
through his chest. He stacked the papers and set one of Lisa's
boxed meals inside the oven, thinking of the neighborhood
boys. That coy, insidious doublespeak. The tauntingly amiable
tone—"she in and out"—moments after the brat flashed his
pawnshop pistol. The Lean Cuisine sizzled. Before its time
arrived, John lumbered down the stairwell.

The boys had vanished. Late afternoon traffic was in motion.
Here and there a suburban ride—Windstars, Volvos—cruised
past. You could drive this strip for years and never turn off into
the neighborhoods to reckon with the truth of the city. For
several minutes John walked east on Grand before cutting onto
Washburn, the side street where the first killings had occurred.
At the corner stood a cement hub, shuttered, decorated with a
cracked barbershop pole. Beyond that came the houses: the
first few with caved-in roofs and another blackened by flame.
Small structures, built in the '50s for families of the steel and
auto plants. There remained one occupied residence for every
six or seven.

He was halfway down the block before realizing he'd never
ventured so deep into the neighborhood. Like any commuter,
he'd acknowledged these passageways only by their rusted signs
posted along the avenue. He'd lived perched on the edge, oblivious to the wreckage back here: yards piled with trash; rusted,
inoperable cars on the street. Where one house had burned to
a heap of shingles, it looked as though someone had been tossing used diapers like softballs onto the carnage—about thirty
white lumps shriveling beneath the sun.

It took more than entertainment districts and running water

and electricity to keep a place alive: something else, for which John had yet to discover a name. Just as the gun-toting boy said, two blocks down Washburn stood a house with yellow-painted iron barricading a porch that stretched the length of its façade. Every visible window was also barred with sulfur-colored metal, though the lawn was trimmed and the address was plain to see.

John walked the steps and pressed the doorbell, rapping twice on the metal enclosure. The porch was swept, tidy. Beyond was the front door, protected by another security gate made of cast iron. He felt the eyes of the block were upon him, peering over sills, watching for the madman, the cops.

The front door opened, though he couldn't see who stood behind the bars.

"I'm looking for a girl. I'm here about the neighborhood watch."

"Who is it?" A young voice.

"I live around the corner."

With the turn of a bolt, the security gate swung forward. Out stepped the dreadlocked girl's silent friend, averred witness to the killer. She wore a pink halter on which an arrangement of rhinestones spelled cutie and a pair of gray sweats. Shuffling toward the bars that encaged the porch, she whispered, "We ain't supposed to be messin'."

"With what? I'm not messing with anything."

"The psycho. We aren't supposed to go messin' around looking for him."

"Okay." He lowered his voice. "But you saw him?"

The girl stared abstractedly, her face coming to rest inches from the bars. John saw now that her nose was malformed,

22

practically flattened, yet she was gorgeous in some creaturely way. Her giant, wet eyes did not appear attuned to the world at large. Hers was the uncertain gaze of a dreamer who couldn't distinguish between her darker fantasies and the cold, harsh facts of what was.

"I know something else," she said.

"What?" John leaned against the wrought iron. The yellow paint was chipped, the metal lattice twirling up to where it was bolted to the brick overhang above.

"I can't show you now," she said.

"Tell me—I'm all right."

A car motored down the street, large and bawdy with thumping bass and tinted windows. The driver didn't brake or seem to take notice, but when John turned back to the girl, her face expressed a new confusion.

"You gonna help us?" she said.

There came a racket from inside the house, a voice John could barely hear.

The girl turned and hollered, "It ain't no one."

"You know where I live," he said. "Above the old flower shop. Just over there."

The girl inched back through the house's doorway, pulling the security gate and turning over its lock. "It's just another man from the newspaper," she said, gazing once more at John. "And we ain't talking."

The room—a second-story bedroom—smelled of wood char and mildew. It was pitch dark but for the faintest light wedging through a two-inch crack near the bottom of an otherwise veiled window. This street was not lit by city taxes—all lamps were burned out. Walking back here had been like trudging some moonless cavern, until John's had eyes had adjusted and he'd seen shadows of the surrounding vacant homes.

It was after two a.m.

All that was left to do was watch.

In rhythm with his pulse John squeezed his tennis ball. Crouching low, peering through the slit at the bottom of the window, he watched a pair of headlamps raying down the street like a yellow genesis, dwindling as the vehicle schussed by. In its wake two low-lit windows in the house across the street appeared to swell. John watched for shapes, shadows. A folding chair sat just behind him, positioned as if to allow for a view beneath the window's shade, which had been fashioned out of a blanket. This, along with a few scuff marks on the sill and an empty tuna can, were alleged evidence of the killer's process.

"Well," John said, the first word he'd spoken since he'd followed the girls here, several blocks into the void. "It doesn't necessarily mean anything."

Hours earlier—nine o'clock or so—as he'd been drifting asleep, Lisa had called. She'd just finished a movie when the sensation overwhelmed her: gratitude that her brother was alive, had come home just in time. "What movie?" he'd asked. "A terrible, hollow story," she'd said. "Where everyone dies. I don't know why I used to love it." Which marked the instant John realized they'd someday leave for a part of this world neither of them had yet to see. Pasadena had been his first thought, a California he knew only through Heidi's tender drawl and sunny ways. Once his strength returned, he'd figure out what it might take. You get eight or so decades at best to find a plot of land where, with any luck, you might live in relative peace, keeping close the things you love. He saw tomatoes blooming in a yard, plucked from the vine and fed to neighbors. He imagined making do with VHS tapes and a television that couldn't be tuned to any channel, he and Lisa escaping the signals, no eyes on them as they strolled sidewalks. These notions had once seemed for quitters but, as if a switch were thrown, he'd given up. Cities had no use for him, not this one. Lisa sensed the shift. Not that he'd confessed; it was plainly obvious when he'd said, "Maybe we try something different." Because she'd sighed deep and said nothing, John knew that she didn't want to chance a single word that might change his mind. Three hours later he'd been startled awake by a knock and leapt from the couch, the dead phone held to his chest.

"How do you figure," he whispered now, "this has anything to do with anything?"

"He's scoping the place," said the girl with the mini-dreads.

She'd pounded on his door and done the talking. Her friend, the mystic-eyed witness, had yet to make a sound. She stood in the shadows, as if to evaporate at the first sign of danger. "This is his hideout," said the girl. "And look." She crouched and pointed across the street, the illuminated windows, shades drawn, a couple of decent cars in the drive. "That there's one bad house."

"You mean dealers?" John said.

He saw her anew, pubescent, the balmy outline of her young face peering beside him. He smelled candy-scented lotion. As she stood, her head rose into darkness. Her friend remained so silent only the twinkle of her rhinestoned shirt convinced him she was still there.

"They running stuff in that house," said the girl. "Those the guys you do not go near."

"No," John said. "Don't go near them."

His knee started up.

"We found a chair like this in a house on Brentwood, right next to where those other guys got killed. We seen the cops nosing around up there. When they left we went and looked and it was the same—a chair and little cuts in the wood, just like here."

"That could be anything," John said, running a finger along the splintered notches.

"This dude be watching before he goes and cuts people up."

"Jesus," John said.

"Don't say that," said the girl.

"What?"

"Don't be cussing that name."

"Sorry," he whispered. "You tell the police about this?"

"We ain't supposed to be messin'. Killer finds out, he'll come for us."

"No. That's not gonna happen."

"Now we telling you," she said. "So you keep a look out."

Her words were spectral, awakening a gravid sense that he'd been given the care of their secret. They'd brought him here, trusting him to be their eyes, that he might witness what they were not meant to.

He sat down in the folding chair—flimsy, dainty for a killer. He'd have worried about bungling the forensics, but the chair seemed an invitation, set there, awaiting him. Hunching slightly forward, he glimpsed again the soft-glowing windows of the house across the street. He stared with pure concentration,

SKRYPTOR

fingering the tennis ball's seams, his knee a piston as he scanned for shadows.

A perfect view, now that he'd taken his seat.

"So, that's it," said the girl. "Get outta here before the devil himself shows."

Squinting, John couldn't turn away from the face of the dreary house. There was the slightest tug of his ponytail—he felt it but didn't turn. A new vehicle rolled down the street, out of view, grumbling softly like a coming storm. Seconds later the van itself appeared. Its headlamps were off. John felt saliva beading on his tongue as he watched the van pull to the curb and heard its engine cut.

"Who's this?" he whispered. "What's happening?" Nothing was visible through the van's windows, least not the presence of a living thing. "Help me look," he said. "Your eyes are better than mine."

When he turned, he saw the girls had vanished and he was alone with the slant of pale light. It rayed across the sill to touch his knee. With one hand he squeezed the ball, bringing the other to his cheek, as if to assure himself of where, precisely, his body was within the room. He felt his blood rush—it was his by now, having traveled every inch of him. He peered again through the crack between the sheet and the sill, just in time to hear the van start up, to see it idling there like whoever was behind the wheel had slipped inside the house and done their business in the blink of an eye—or as though they'd had a premonition, warning them to get a move on, knowing someone was watching from above.

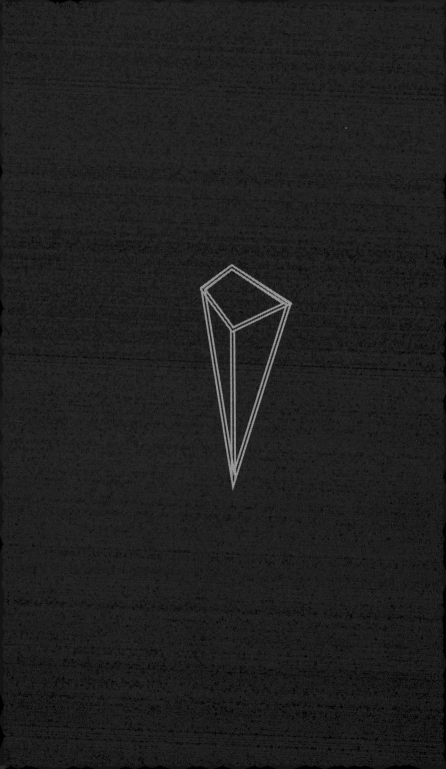

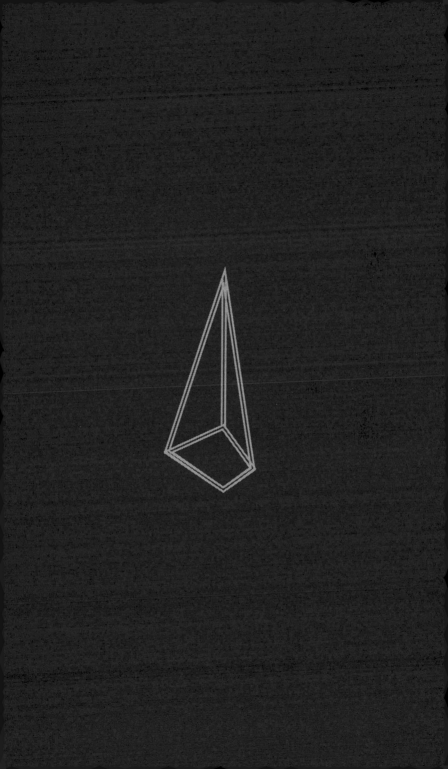

Fritz Welch

DAVID MᶜCLELLAND

Dry Cleaning

He had to buy new clothes for his new job, but now that he had
a job, he could afford the clothes. The new clothes needed to be
dry-cleaned, and when he came home and undressed after the
third day at his new job his skin was tender and pink where it
had been touched by the dry-cleaned clothes. He could see the
cuff lines and the stitching of his shirt like a sewing pattern
imprinted on his skin. His forearms were swollen and itchy.
He took a shower, but the heat made the itching and puffiness
worse, so he took some aspirin and went to bed.

In the morning he felt as if he were lying on the points of
needles, and he could barely sit up. He slowly got out of bed and
went to the bathroom and looked in the mirror. His skin was
puffy, and mottled pink and white. His face was like a drawing
on a big pink marble, and his fingers had become so thick that
he could barely separate them. With a great deal of effort he
manipulated the telephone and called his job and left a message
that he wouldn't be in to work that day. His voice sounded dim

and muffled to his own ears. He tried to reach his doctor but no one answered, and he left a message there as well. He took a sheet from the closet and wrapped it loosely around himself so he wouldn't have to keep seeing what had happened to his genitals. He tried his doctor again, and this time spoke with his doctor's secretary, and she called an ambulance to come and get him.

He sat in his kitchen chair and waited. The ambulance didn't arrive. Before it had driven a block from the hospital it was stopped by a garbage truck filling up with appliances and broken wallboard and black plastic bags of debris from a building renovation. The ambulance sat there with its siren cycling up and down until one of the garbage men came over and tapped a box cutter against the windshield. The driver rolled down his window and the garbage man stood on the step-up of the ambulance and reached in and took hold of the driver's neck, with his thumb pressing hard against the man's larynx. "Turn it off," the garbage man said. The driver let the siren fade. In the quiet afterward someone ran out from the hospital and told the other medic that his wife was calling, she was finally going into labor, and the medic jumped out of the ambulance and ran up the street to Lexington Avenue and flagged down a taxicab and got in and was driven away.

The man waiting in his kitchen never learned all this. He felt worse and worse. He was becoming hungry in a concentrated way that verged on nausea. He poured himself a bowl of cereal and milk but he could barely fit the spoon between his swollen lips, and having food in his mouth made him fear he might choke. His skin felt tighter and tighter and more and more itchy. When he moved his arms the taut skin at his elbows and knuckles sparkled with a pain like clusters of tiny razor cuts. His heart was speeding along like the heart of a tiny frightened animal. His eyelids pushed themselves closed. He sat in the itchy darkness and felt a tickling on his chest. He touched himself carefully and found that his chest was wet. The wetness on his chest was warm and sticky. His fingers discovered an opening in his chest. He pulled at its edges, and the more he pulled, the more the tightness of his skin was relieved. The darkness at his eyes gave way and he could see the kitchen through a wet, reddish haze. He pulled at both sides of the opening, pulling it wide, and stepped out of his skin as if he were stepping out of an unzipped jumpsuit.

His skin sat in the kitchen chair, and without him inside it did not look particularly swollen. The split he had stepped out of started at what had been his throat and ran vertically down the length of the skin body. He pushed the edges of the split together and straightened the empty body until it looked like a person sitting in the kitchen chair with his eyes closed. Like himself sitting there in the kitchen chair, with his eyes closed.

As he was doing this he saw his hands. They were small now, bluish white and deeply wrinkled, like the grooved shell of a walnut, if walnuts were the blue-white of ice cubes, and smeared red and greasy with fat and blood. He walked to the bathroom and his feet made wet sounds on the linoleum floor. His chest was at the level of the bathroom sink, and he could see only the top of his head in the mirror. The hair there looked unfamiliar and strange—stiff and wiry—but it was his hair, for it moved when he moved. He got in the shower and washed off the blood and greasy fat. The deep wrinkles ran unbroken down his arms and legs and belly, his genitals were shrunken and hard, and his toes were shriveled nubs, with gray toenails like small, pointy rocks buried in the flesh.

After he toweled off he stood carefully on the toilet seat and leaned across the bathroom sink to look at himself in the mirror. He saw his face, and his eyes. He looked into his own eyes for quite a while. Then he got off the toilet and got back into his bed and pulled the covers to his neck and closed his eyes and died.

Later that morning the man made out of empty skin opened his eyes and got up from his kitchen seat and went to the bathroom sink and wet a towel and used it to wipe the smears of blood from his chest, where the vertical slit had seamed over completely. He combed his hair with his fingers and turned his head to look at himself in profile and frowned and smiled and coughed and clapped his hands. His hands hung loosely on his wrists and looked limp and a bit flabby and made a funny flapping sound when he clapped. He pressed on himself at different places and watched the impressions of his fingers push in and then after a moment smooth out.

"Well," he said. "I need a bit of stuff in there. I'll have to see about that."

He was dressing himself when the doorbell rang. He opened the door to a man and a woman, both in dark blue EMT clothing, carrying bags of medical equipment. The woman had a clipboard in her hand. "We had a call," she said.

"I'm so sorry," the man said as he buttoned a clean white shirt over his undershirt. "I did call my doctor earlier. But the situation's passed. Really nothing to worry about now. I mean, look at me now. Does anything look wrong?"

He showed them his profile, smiled for them. The man and woman in the doorway looked at him, frowning.

He said, "Absolutely normal, don't you think? And now I have to get ready for my new job."

"Thing is," the woman said. "We should give you a once-over, probably. Blood tests, heart rate. Make sure everything's okay."

"I really don't think that's necessary," the man said. "The only thing I've got is butterflies in my stomach, and that's just excitement. New job."

The woman took notes on her clipboard. "So you're refusing medical treatment."

"If you put it like that, I suppose I am."

"Medical treatment offered. Subject refused. Visual examination only."

"And I look normal, don't I? Absolutely normal."

The male EMT said something under his breath, and he and the woman went away under the fluorescent lights of the apartment building's dingy hallway.

The receptionist at his new job was surprised to see him, but he told her that he was feeling much better, thank you. On the way to his desk he stopped at the supply closet and took out two reams of paper and two boxes of unsharpened pencils. He sat at the desk in his cubicle and turned on his computer and logged in. He opened a ream of paper and balled up the top sheet and put it in his mouth and chewed and swallowed it down. After chewing and swallowing a few more sheets he opened a box of pencils and took one out and put the end of it in his mouth and sucked it down. He did this again and again, slowly and methodically as he worked at his desk, and after an hour he got up and went to the bathroom. He walked across the room, waving hello to his new coworkers. In the bathroom, he looked at himself in the mirror. Turned so he could see his profile. Smiled, frowned, pulled at his ears. Ran his fingers through his hair. Everything seemed well attached. He reached down and felt his ankles, his knees. Feeling less hollow down there. More solid. Someone had left a lighter on the bathroom counter, and he ate it. He went back to his desk and back to chewing and swallowing sheets of paper and sucking down pencils.

At the end of the day, Wendy, the human resources director, knocked on the door of one of the corner offices.

"Bob," she said. "Sorry to bother. You know the new guy, right?"

The man in the office looked up from his desk.

"In data reclamation? Sure. Gave him his intake interview. Problem?"

"Well. Today. He calls in sick, but then he shows up, which, okay. But now he's just sitting there."

"Sitting there?"

"I mean, won't respond when you talk to him. Not working. Just sitting there."

"He called in sick? On what, his third day?"

"But then he came in anyway. And now, I don't know. He won't answer me. I thought, maybe..."

Bob said, "Talk to him? Glad to."

They went through the aisles of cubicles to the man's desk and found him sitting with both hands on his keyboard, looking at his dark computer screen.

"Hey there," Bob said. "Just wanted to stop by and see how it's going for you."

No answer.

Bob put a hand on the man's shoulder but then took it away quickly. The head of the man at the desk nodded forward, and then the shoulders slumped, and his entire body slid forward and down so that his face was on the keyboard and his arms were pushed across the desk, his elbows and wrists and fingers all twisted and bent at unlikely angles.

"Call an ambulance," Bob said.

Wendy went away. Bob stood there saying, "Bud, hey Bud." The smell of grilling beef rose up off the body. Bob took a step back. A small colorless flame began burning at the top of the man's head, and as it burned into his hair and skin it gave off a black smoke. Patches of brown bloomed on the man's white shirt and charred black as flames ate through the fabric. The flames traveled rapidly across the slumped body and caught the papers on the desk. The computer monitor began to discolor and become oily and slick in the melting heat. Soon the entire cubicle was a box of flames lashing at the ceiling. The other office workers began shouting and fled toward the elevators and stairs. Bob ran for the fire extinguisher and pulled the safety ring and unclipped the black nozzle and pointed it at the flames and squeezed the handle, but it gave out only a single ball of white vapor. In the middle of the flames and black smoke the shape of the man showed clearly, head down at his desk as if he were napping. Papers tacked to the walls of the cubicle were lifting and curling into ash. The sprinkler system came on, hissing loudly, and soon everything on the entire floor was wet and dripping, but the man at the desk kept burning.

By the time the firemen arrived the body had burned itself away. The sprinkler system and the flame-retardant cubicle walls had kept the fire from spreading. The firemen stood in their yellow suits and hats, carrying their axes, and looked into the burnt box of the cubicle. Everything in it was black and the texture of wet charcoal. The burning body had bitten a half circle out of the desk top, and the computer monitor was a blackened lump with a shattered screen. The chair had melted down to its steel base. There was an insistent chemical smell mixed with a barbecue odor, the smell of cooking fat. All that was left of the man who had caught fire were his footprints traced into the burned carpet.

"That desk's a write-off," one of the firemen said.

He had called his mother the day he was hired. He told her that she was right, that life in the city was never going to be easy, but that he had found a new job, and she should come for a visit and see how well he was doing. He told her to bring a dress so he could take her someplace nice for a nice dinner. He told her he would pay for the bus ticket, for the taxis, for the dinner, everything.

At the end of what would have been his fourth day at his new job his mother got out of a taxi in front of his building and pressed his apartment buzzer, but there was no answer. The intercom buttons seemed not to be connected to anything. She saw that the building door was open, that the lock was broken and jammed, and she went in and walked slowly up the two flights of stairs to her son's apartment and knocked. No answer. She tried the handle and the door opened. She put her bag by the front door and went through the small apartment, calling her son's name and turning on the lights as she went.

In the bedroom she saw a little mound under the bedcovers. She said her son's name. She turned down the covers to reveal the small pale shape, wrinkled and curled up on itself, its knees touching its elbows and its hands at its face, eyes closed. She sat on the edge of the bed and put her hand on one of the small hard feet.

"There you are," she said.

TOM NEWTON

The Sound of the Bridge

I have a large table which seats ten, so when I have the occasional dinner party there are ten guests—usually the same people.

But recently there was a newcomer, Ian Waters. Liz had invited him. He was older than the rest of us. He was seated at the head of the table and I sat next to him.

Though nominally master of my own house I eschewed the custom of taking the head of the table. It was too formal. Maybe I should have got a round table like King Arthur but I didn't have the space for it. Anyway I lived alone so these cumbersome traditions were irrelevant.

Whenever I had people over I always took the chair on the side, next to the head of the table. The occupant of that position always seemed separated from the rest. And that was the case with Ian. There was something odd about him, though I couldn't tell what it was. He seemed normal enough—gracious and friendly, easily engaging in conversation.

Aside from a little small talk, I preferred to avoid conversations at my dinner parties. I would rise constantly from my chair to attend to the food and wine, letting the others amuse themselves. It might seem paradoxical to invite people over and be unwilling to talk to them but I liked it that way. I just listened.

The talk had turned to memory—specifically the idea seemingly corroborated by modern science that in order to recall a memory it had to be reinvented. There was some kind of mechanism involving certain proteins which was beyond me, as I'm sure it was everyone else. But it opened up all kinds of possibilities and questions. If a memory had to be constantly reinvented then was it really a memory? Was it the same each time it was recalled? Maybe there was no such thing as memory. But then what? Could you say that nothing happened?

"Of course things happen."

"But without memory, you can never be sure."

Then Ian began to speak. He had a friend, he said, who he would leave nameless. It didn't matter much anyway as none of us knew him.

I wondered how he could be so sure of that.

This man he mentioned was a sound engineer. Quite a successful one. He'd had a hand in many records that were probably familiar to all of us.

Ian was a good storyteller. That was apparent. Other conversations around the table trailed off as all attention was turned to him.

"He told me that a few months ago he was sitting in his car underneath the Queensborough Bridge in New York, on the Queens side. He had some time to kill and decided to use it by listening to the bridge."

"That's a cool idea."

"Yes. He described to me the sounds he heard. 'Monstrous' was the word he used."

"It's amazing how we can shut out the sounds of the city. We're probably in 'fight' mode all the time without realizing it. Can't be good. All that stress and adrenaline."

"Well the sounds he told me about—the screeching and groaning, the banging and the ceaseless roar of traffic had an unexpected effect on him."

"What was that?"

"An image began to form clearly in his mind, seemingly out of nowhere. An image of water. But it wasn't pleasant or relaxing like the ocean crashing onto a beach. No, it was still water, dark and stagnant. Very still. And the thing is, once he had seen that image he couldn't get rid of it. No matter where he went or what he did, it stayed in his mind. Even sleep provided no relief. It infused his dreams.

"After a few weeks this obsession began to take its toll. I met him at that time and that's when he told me what had been going on. He seemed to be in a state of nervous exhaustion, or hyper-anxiety, or whatever it's called these days. He had trouble concentrating and had completely lost his appetite. He said he was going to get medical help.

"He went to a number of specialists and they ran a gamut of tests. Initially they had suspected a brain tumor. He had several MRIs but there was nothing abnormal as far as they could tell. In the end the best they could come up with was that he was suffering from panic attacks. Though, from what he had read about it, he didn't think that his condition fit the diagnosis. It wasn't something that went away and came back. It was there the whole time—an onslaught. They prescribed him some pills to calm him down but the image remained. It was a good thing he had health insurance as I'm sure it cost a fortune. He had coverage through his wife—the music business is not known for providing benefits. She's done quite well for herself. She is the dean of some prestigious college."

Ian was beginning to lose his thread. The attention around the table faltered. But then I had the feeling that his rambling about doctors and medicine was deliberate. He was using some kind of oratorical punctuation, preparing his audience for what was to follow.

He disturbed me. More so because I did not know why.

"Maybe the medication did work after all. It might have calmed him enough to think more clearly. Either way, soon after that he got the idea that this persistent image was a memory that manifested itself in an unusual way. Once he had come to that realization—if that's what it was, he had a direction to follow and felt some relief. That was short-lived though, because he started seeing a submerged face. Sometimes it was there and sometimes not. Perhaps he saw strands of hair floating in the dark water. If this was a memory, it was not a good one."

Liz interrupted. "What did his wife make of it?"

A flicker of irritation crossed Ian's eyes, but it was momentary, as the passing shadow of a cloud.

"That's complicated. They'd been married a long time but they'd never got along. I've often wondered why they stayed together. It could be that they both derived some mutual benefit from perpetual disagreement and resentment... Anyway, once he had suspected this image was a memory, he began to search for it. The recurring face haunted him but no matter how hard he tried, he couldn't remember anything.

"We assume without thinking that our memories belong to us. We can recall them at will and make whatever use of them we choose. So imagine his condition. It was a disintegration, an alienation that separated him from everything he thought he knew and left him as a mere object acted upon by a senseless existence.

"Accepting that he had reached a dead end, he took another approach. He tried to enlarge the picture—to see more detail, hoping that he would find something that would trigger his memory and that all would be revealed.

"He saw that the water was contained in a rusted metal tank that stood above ground. He looked beyond it and saw trees. Unruly, unkempt.

"It could be an old cistern for collecting rainwater, he thought. Somewhere rural. A tank like that might have been the water supply for a cabin in the woods. A hunting cabin perhaps. He realized he couldn't visualize the cabin because as the observer of this image, it would be behind him. But he felt he was getting somewhere at last and wracked his brain for a memory of such a place."

"So tell me, Ian, how do you know so much about all this?"

Paddy sat at the other end of the table. He was a naysayer, always skeptical, and seemed to enjoy picking holes in other people's statements. I wondered if he had been like that as a child. Ian had met his match, I thought.

But Ian was not thrown. He glanced down the table and countered with, "I imagine you are aware of empathy..." Then he picked up where he had left off.

"With a jolt he remembered his wife telling him that her grandparents had owned some land in Greene County. They had built a small cabin, where they would go to escape the summer heat in the city. She had never liked the place. As far as he knew, it was still in the family but he couldn't recall ever going there himself. Still, he felt he had found a piece of the puzzle. It was a starting point.

"Maybe it was no coincidence that now that he had fixed a location for his vision he saw the body again, face up, just beneath the surface. Pale with strands of hair that gently undulated in the still water as if by Brownian motion. He stared with a growing horror at what was before him.

"With constant, gnawing introspection, he came to the conclusion that he had killed someone and deliberately forgotten about it, or repressed it. That thought, now unleashed, took hold of him with frenetic abandon. He examined his entire life as much as he could remember it, searching for a victim and a motive.

"There had been a time when he was younger when things had been much more volatile. That was when he still believed in what he did and in the products he made. He had lived the life, to the hilt. But it all seemed so murky now and offered up no clues.

"He was going to have to find that cabin and take a look for himself. That was the only way he would know whether this vision was a repressed memory or not. He would search

SKRYPTOR

that tank. He pondered that he might be an unwitting psychic receiving information on another's crime. But that was unlikely—wishful thinking, perhaps. His gut told him that he was the culprit.

"He wondered about the best way to get the address. His wife must have it. Should he be straightforward with her, or circumspect? He decided to be honest and tell her what he planned to do. She knew what he had been going through and was probably as exasperated as he was.

"The trouble was, when he asked her one morning before she left for work, she couldn't remember it. She had been a child when she went there last. And she had always hated the place. She didn't even know if it was still standing. Her grandfather had built it and he was a cheapskate.

"In the end, with assistance from relatives, she was able to provide it. The cabin still existed as far as anyone knew.

"He picked a Thursday to drive up there. Days of the week didn't mean much to him, not working an orthodox job, but he wanted to avoid the weekend traffic.

"He traveled light—his GPS, a shovel, wire cutters, rain gear, a bag of nuts and a gallon of water. As an afterthought he took the pearl-handled revolver, given to him by a music promoter many years before that had languished in a drawer ever since.

"It took just over three hours to get there. Traffic was heavy in the city but thinned out as he drove further north. He found himself on a dirt road leading deep into the woods. It was barely drivable and confused his GPS. Its female voice told him to turn around as soon as possible. But he kept going and reached it at last—if it was indeed the right place.

"He turned off the car and sat for a while. Outside there was a light drizzle. The trees glistened with dampness. Everywhere around him there was decay. It was as prevalent as growth. He was staring at a constant process of death and regeneration and it all appeared completely motionless. It was a similar perception of scale that allowed a person to stand on the world and be unaware of its rotation. The fallen branches and the beds of leaves were striking in their complexity. Everything was rotting.

"He turned his eyes to the cabin in front of him. It was small and appeared to be L-shaped. There was a storm door of corroded aluminum, pockmarked with age and flecked with the white dots of oxidization. As his eyes roved over the building and noticed the mildew creeping up onto the walls from the ground he realized that his powers of observation had become honed. In equal measure his obsessive search for a memory had receded. But that cloying, clawing feeling had been replaced with fear. It was time to do what he had come there for.

"He got out of the car and peered through a small window into the cabin. Windows so minuscule would not be acceptable these days. It made him understand how different life was in the past, and how much was now taken for granted.

"He couldn't see clearly; it was dark inside. He swung open the storm door and tried the main door. It was unlocked. Cautiously he stepped in.

"The first thing he noticed was the strong smell of mold. Immediately to his right was a room. Probably it was once a bedroom. He wondered what people had found to do there all summer. Ahead of him was a short, narrow corridor that led into what he presumed was the kitchen. Beyond that was another claustrophobic bedroom.

"Halfway along the corridor, on the left side, was a closet with an open sliding door. A pile of shoes lay tumbled from it on the floor in a haphazard fashion.

"It was an eerie sight. Why so many shoes in a place like this? They suggested a sudden and unplanned exodus, a moment of panic that had lasted for years. He had a strong sense of those anonymous feet that had once worn those shoes yet departed without them. What could have caused them to do that? Everything that had happened echoed through time.

"Next to the closet was another door. This was the bathroom. So they hadn't used an outhouse as he would have expected. Maybe the bathroom was added later. He stared in. There was a stained toilet with a cracked seat, and on the wall next to it a metal medicine cabinet with no door. A few cloudy glass bottles stood on the shelves, connected to each other with spiderwebs. A bathtub stretched along the other wall, filled with building detritus—broken planks, cardboard and rolls of mildewed wallpaper.

"It didn't take him long to finish his exploration of the cabin, and he was relieved to go back outside. He had been looking for something to jolt his memory, but beyond the shoes and the ubiquitous evidence of mice and spiders, nothing else had caught his eye.

"The jumble of shoes was jarring but it didn't provide him with any of the details he had hoped for, only a disconcerting feeling that just exacerbated his sense of foreboding.

"Outside, the drizzle kept coming. The sky was opaque and oppressive. It kept secrets and gave nothing away. He pulled up the hood of his anorak and walked around to the back of the building.

"And there it was, just as he had seen it. The rusted metal tank sat on a concrete slab about thirty feet away. He hadn't noticed the slab in his vision but the trees were the same. They were smaller than most of the others in the forest. The area had obviously been cleared once and they had been encroaching on it ever since in a gradual but relentless process of reclamation. Broken wood lay scattered randomly across the landscape, like the shoes outside the closet.

"The tank stood about four feet tall. Its rim had corroded in some areas, leaving jagged holes reminiscent of maps of unknown coastlines.

"With trepidation he peered over the edge. Leaves were suspended in the dark water, clustered in the corners. He was relieved not to see a floating corpse but he knew that he had to be certain, so he went back to the car and got the shovel. He started to churn the water with it but it wasn't long enough to probe the depths. He looked around and found a piece of electrical conduit. It was hard work pulling it out of the ground. Eventually he carried it back to the tank and poked around in the foul water.

"More leaves rose to the surface, dark and slimy, releasing a powerful odor. It was the peculiar and unpleasant smell of things that rot in water. He splashed himself a few times in the process and recoiled in disgust. A dead frog rose up, slowly gyrating. It was bloated and almost translucent. As it floated away from him, he felt as if he were watching a Danse Macabre.

"At every prod he became more tense, knowing that soon he

would come across the person he had killed and then he would have to face himself. Who was this person he had brought here and held down in this water? And why? After years of ignorance he would have to shoulder the responsibility for what he had done. He would stagger beneath it wherever it might lead him, but at least he would know himself. This half-life existence of dream and supposition would be over. It was driving him mad.

"Ten fraught minutes of searching finally convinced him that there was no human body in the tank. He stood back and threw down the pipe. Nothing he had seen explained the image that had plagued him, but now he knew that he had not committed murder.

"He turned his back on the tank and walked into the woods. He wanted to see if that wretched vision remained in his mind. It was gone. He had exorcised himself.

"As he aimlessly put distance between himself and the cabin, he felt the anxiety that had consumed him for so long dissolve into the forest. It gave him the sensation of clarity. He was able to see all the recent events in his life and the strands that bound them to one another. The metallic sounds of the bridge, the sounds of inorganic pain, the metal tank, the water it contained, the face beneath the water, the fear and pain and loneliness of drowning. The meaning that lingered in a pile of shoes. The dissipation of all things.

"That feeling of clarity was just a moment. It passed quickly as twigs snapped beneath his feet and brambles snared his clothes. His intentions passed along with it. There was no need to make sense of anything. All that remained was the entropic process of growth and decay.

"Relief takes different guises. For him I think it was a flowing-out, an emptying."

Ian sat back in his chair and sipped from his glass. Everyone else relaxed. I had found his monologue overbearing. It seemed to be an unreasonable demand for attention and left me wondering about his purpose, because I was sure he had one. I scraped back my chair and headed for the kitchen. I could hear their voices from my refuge. Paddy was talking.

"Interesting story. But I imagine that's all it is, a story, right?"

I could hear Ian's mellifluous voice in response.

"We were talking about memory. Isn't that just what a memory is? A story, or a series of them?"

"It sounds to me like you were talking about yourself. Are they your memories you've been telling us?"

That was the other Iain, the one with the extra "I" in his name. His parents had probably added it in a nod to their Gaelic ancestry. He was someone who always appeared to consider what he was about to say before speaking.

"Well yes, they are my memories but only inasmuch as they are what I remember about someone else's memories. But it's possible that I might just be reinventing them." He chuckled.

"But you went from describing someone else's memories to becoming that person yourself."

"I was telling a story. Isn't that what we do in stories—wear the shoes of our characters? Empathize, as I was saying."

I missed what followed as I had turned on the tap to rinse a glass and it momentarily drowned out the conversation. I was happy to be free of it for a while. It had left me feeling uneasy. Then I heard Jane speaking.

"So what became of your friend? Did he recover?"

"I can't really say."

"What do you mean? You don't know?"

"Well you see, he never returned from that trip upstate. Maybe he's in the hospital, or perhaps he ran off somewhere and started a new life. I don't know what became of him. But I'm sure he'll resurface sooner or later."

"You don't seem too worried."

"Worry doesn't accomplish much, does it?

And then I heard Paddy chime in again, in his accusatory style.

"Would you say that memories are limited to the past? Could there not be a memory of something that has not yet happened?"

"That would be precognition, wouldn't it?"

"I'm not sure there's a difference."

I came back to the table to clear it. Liz was leaning in toward Ian, looking at him earnestly, conspiratorially almost.

"Haven't you spoken to his wife?"

She struck me as overly concerned about this man's wife. What was it to her? It annoyed me. All the more so since Ian was her friend and she was the one who had invited him to my house. "You don't mind if I bring a friend along?" She had asked me. "He's an interesting guy."

That might be but he wouldn't be coming back again, as far as I was concerned.

Ian didn't reply right away. He seemed lost for words, or distracted by his own thoughts. The confidence he had displayed earlier with so little effort now seemed less strident.

"Spoken to her? Yes of course. We moved in together recently."

Guno Park

WILLIAM A. TURLEY

Memories

PURCHASE ORDER—RUSH (12/01/17):

28 @ 1m x 7m x 5cm glasspanels, aquarium grade
28 @ reinforced aluminum separators, 7m length
875 bags dry concrete
9 @ pumps, 1 hp, electric or gas
10,000 kg marine salt mix
33 under-gravel aquarium heaters
High-capacity reverse osmosis pump

APPROVED NOTE:

Alex,

By my quick calculations, this is a 300k liter tank (!?) You have the budget, but this will eat up 75% of what's remaining for this year. Please let me know if there is anything misunderstood.

—Deborah

P.S.: You didn't include lights or electricals. Ask Jesus if you need help with setup.

ABSTRACT, A. PIROPOLOUS, ET AL.:

The Larger Pacific Octopus (as yet unnamed cousin of Octopus Chierchiae) is the subject of many studies on the presence of creative intelligence in cephalopods, including anecdotal (*see 1 and 16*) and experimental (*see 2–15*) evidence. In this program, the aim is to test the baseline, instinctive abilities compared to adult behavior. Several sub-programs and experiments are described within.

Given the relatively short lifespan of the octopus species, it is unclear how learned behavior is obtained and integrated in individuals. This program intends to demonstrate that the innate, instinctive behavior of the representative octopus species is sufficient to explain most so-called learned behaviors in the genus.

SKRYPTOR

NOTES, UNDATED (*The following, and all subsequent "Notes, undated" in this file were transcribed from the audio files of subject—Dr. A Piropolous [AP]—post-incident of 12/19/17, encrypted; discovered on private server 3/03/18. Excerpts of the following were copied on public server owned by the Aquatic Institute.*):

AP: My plan to begin with a breeding colony of eleven individuals seems to be successful. The first brood, roughly twenty-eight viable eggs, have been relocated with the mother to tank three. The social nature of the species has pros and cons. The fact that they will tolerate one another well in relatively close proximity makes normal upkeep simpler. However, we didn't envision having to move an aggressive female to the brood tank with the eggs, so we had to make last minute adjustments.

BREAK FORMAL NOTE; PRIVATE

Actually, it was something of a disaster. We lost well over half of the eggs and injured the mother, causing distress. Jesus was also injured, but it's superficial. It looked to me like he was clumsy, but he insists that he was pulled into the edge of the tank. The broken glass took the emergency room staff at least 30 minutes to remove from his triceps, and he required several sets of stitches. The most alarming aspect was that the males crowded around while we helped him out of the tank, like they were attracted to his blood. We have never seen that behavior in cephalopod species before, more commonly found in sharks.

So far, the preliminary steps have gone as expected. Our comparison species Sepia Officinalis—common cuttlefish—met my expectations completely. Dr. Galvez's comparison of cuttles to bonobos and octos to chimpanzees was startlingly accurate. Cuttlefish really do behave like easygoing octopus. It's a little hard not to get attached. We had success with the activity sequence; they worked through the maze sequence with roughly the same level of success as the common rat, as predicted by Galvez's previous studies. I really do hope Jesus is alright. His arm looked like meat before we got into the ER.

Tomorrow, we were scheduled to begin work with the other octos, but that will need to be put off for a day or two. This won't put us behind, since we need to wait for gestation of the youngsters before we really get going. I want to get a baseline for adult behavior, how quickly they pick up new, learned behavior, so I need to observe their resting personalities.

I will have to take care of the DNA sequencing tomorrow, since Jesus will be out for the day.
END PRIVATE NOTE.

NOTES, UNDATED:

AP: DNA sequencing complete on all eleven adults. There seems to be a greater-than average variability among these individuals than among wild-caught samples. It is possible that the supply house sent us an extra-large Lesser Pacific, but I doubt it. The incident of yesterday appears to have been forgotten by the animals. Their color and behavior all seemed within normal parameters. We will continue with the activity sequence tomorrow.

BREAK FORMAL NOTE; PRIVATE.

I am going to spend most of the evening on the phone with our Nicaragua suppliers tonight. I can't believe they sent us a mixed batch of octos. That's the only reasonable explanation for the DNA results. I mean, according to these averages, some of them aren't even the same genera, much less the same species. It won't really matter, once we identify the outliers during our activity testing. Our brood is a pure stock since we hatched them ourselves, assuming that we can get them to adulthood.

Jesus worked a little this afternoon. He didn't want to complete the DNA sequence since he's on painkillers for his arm. It does look a lot better, but he was complaining of residual pain. **END PRIVATE NOTE.**

NOTES, UNDATED:

AP: Dr. Galvez has recused himself from the study. His impact has been immeasurable and his experience will be missed. We began the day two protocol with the eggs, subjecting ten of them to daily doses of UV light. The control group was subjected to a similar amount of time of increased-intensity daylight from the artificial lamps. Resting behavior observations continue on the ten adults remaining in the large tank.

AP: BREAK FORMAL NOTE; PRIVATE.

I cannot believe Jesus quit! He is so levelheaded, normally. Even the painkillers don't explain his behavior. He was nervous getting back to working with the animals, but there was no incident. Then, when I prepared the UV light for the ten hatchlings, he completely lost it. He was complaining about his eyes and had to go lie down. Then he came barging into the brood room and nearly attacked me. He gave no reasonable excuse for his behavior. I don't even know where he went! It can't be that he had some bizarre attack of conscience. He invented the blinding procedure that we use on the embryos. Once the ten little ones hatch, we will be able to put them through their paces, and I am sure that we will show the same innate behaviors as the adults and the control group. They won't be affected by their handicap, and it will prove that octopus behavior can be ascribed to instinct and nothing more.
END PRIVATE NOTE.

EMAIL (*DATED 11/20/17, presumably the day following Dr. Galvez's departure*):
Deborah,
As you know, Dr. Jesus Galvez has left the institute for personal reasons. Unfortunately, he was an invaluable member of our staff and critical to several operations. We need to meet at your earliest convenience to begin the search for his replacement.

—Alex.

RESPONSE (*DATED 11/20/17*):

Alex,

Please keep me in the loop. I trust your judgement concerning staff, so feel free to continue without consulting me.

Thanks!

—Deborah

ABSTRACT, A. PIROPOLOUS, ET AL.:

In sub-program 2 of the experiment (see related notes on other sub-programs), recently hatched embryo of Larger Pacific Octopus (cousin of Octopus Chierchiae) are subjected in ovum to UV light of sufficient intensity to cause blindness. The handicapped individuals are then put through activity series, including mazes, etc. (details in Appendix C). A control group is compared to the test group on the same activity series.

The intent of this sub-program is to establish that cephalopod intelligence is innate and unlearned. Aspects of this study are based on previous experiments administered by Dr. Jesus Galvez, wherein the subject species seemed to display an ability to pass on learned behavior to offspring. The only explanation for such changes is that the behavior was previously unobserved in the adults. Therefore, we decided to compare untested young with both cohort individuals that were not handicapped and the adult/parent generation. Dr. Galvez is unavailable to work with the present study, even though the design is based on his work.

The following parts of the project—sub-programs 3, 3a and 4 through 7—depend upon these steps as a baseline. Future generations, bred from the 10 blinded octos, will be tested against similar individuals bred from the remaining healthy individuals. Sub-program 3 begins once the blind octos are bred and subsequent baseline tests performed. Sub-programs 4 through 7 will include further studies with the third generation and crossbred with the parent generation to ensure genetic variability.

NOTES, UNDATED:

AP: The baby octos are sufficiently mature to begin activity-series testing. Both blind and sighted individuals will be tested simultaneously to ensure that conditions are as similar as possible. I do not share the same doubts as Jesus—Dr. Galvez—that we discussed during our early sessions. While it is highly unlikely that the coincidences identified by Jesus are in any way related to his outcomes, we are actively controlling against them in this round.

END FORMAL NOTE; PERSONAL

The incredible hoops that we will jump through in order to ensure that each round is set up exactly as the others will be a hindrance to completing more than three rounds in a day. This gives us a very short period to work with and a small sample size of individual rounds, which concerns me. However, there will be no doubt: Any learned behavior will be from genetic changes passed down from the parent generation, and not from any other coincidence. Jesus's ludicrous ideas that octos learn at an incredibly fast rate, or that genetic change occurs "by choice," as he put it, needs to be laid to rest. Even he agreed that this step is necessary.

END PRIVATE NOTE.

NOTES, UNDATED:

AP: Preliminary tests complete, with evidence suggesting no difference between the blinded and normal individuals. There is no doubt that the evidence backs my theory that cephalopod intelligence is entirely innate.

Dr. Galvez will be rejoining our program within two weeks. His experience will be a great enhancement to the program's success.

END FORMAL NOTE; PERSONAL

I will not have Jesus working alone with the adult octos. He was too unstable during the previous round, and I cannot have him jeopardizing the data that we have accumulated. It is clear that his theory is almost completely debunked, which may be a blow to his professional standing. However, he enlisted my help with this program just for that purpose. He seems prepared to continue the work, and he still insists that the next generation will vindicate him, but I have my doubts that is possible.
END PRIVATE NOTE.

EMAIL, DATED (12/06/17:)

Alex,

I understand your objections to Dr. Galvez's return to the institute. However, he is clearly recovered from his brief episode of earlier this year. You are welcome to file a protest with HR. Please cc both myself and my director, Dr. Ravishandra, on any communications.

On a personal note, I am surprised at your actions. You fail to understand that all of us—you included—may suffer the indignity of stress and overwork. Have a heart and please try to ease Jesus's return to the team in any way you can. I seem to remember that it was your recommendation that convinced the institute to reach out to Dr. Galvez originally, based on his previous research quality.

—Deborah

RESPONSE:

Deborah,

Noted. I will include you on all communication.

—Alex

NOTES, UNDATED:

AP: Dr. Galvez continues excellent observations with the various adult cephalopod populations. His detailed notes are being compiled in a separate publication detailing normal behavior in a captive population.

END FORMAL NOTE; PRIVATE

Jesus continues to surprise me. He has returned with the same zeal that he showed previously. He seems completely unphased by the episode surrounding his leaving the program and the institute. In fact, I have seen some evidence that he is repressing memories of the episode; at times he seems to forget why or how he injured his arm.

The second generation adult octos are fully integrated into the parent group, now that they are fully mature. There was little difficulty in arranging them among the various tanks. The brood tank will be repurposed over the next weeks while

we await the early phases of ovodepositing. This should begin very soon, based on the pH change evident.
END PRIVATE NOTE.

NOTES, UNDATED:

AP: The second generation octos have mated successfully. Ovodepositing took place today. Interestingly, both the control and blinded population bred on the same day, even though they are isolated. Perhaps this should be considered further evidence of innate behavior.

NOTES, UNDATED:

AP: Day-two protocol was briefly interrupted. There appears to be a phenotypic change to the offspring that Dr. Galvez believes is significant. However, the first round of UV light was administered this afternoon. The delay was not more than three hours, as compared to the first testing group, so the effect is minimal.

END FORMAL NOTE; PRIVATE.

Jesus is cracking up again. That is the only explanation. He was extremely disturbed and refused to continue the experiment, even though he was the one to originally insist on our strict adherence to a similar timeline for all test groups. I cannot imagine that three hours will make any difference to the octo development, even in such a short period as forty-eight hours.

Jesus insists that the offspring have developed a thick eye covering in ovum, similar to an eyelid, that is opaque to visible light. Such a development is impossible. The Large Pacific

Octopus normally develops eyelids after day twenty in ovum. He tried to convince Deborah to shut down the experiments until the protocol can be reviewed! For ethical reasons! Over eyelids.

The worst part of his betrayal is that Deborah is listening to his rantings. He is convinced that the generation-two octos learned what had caused their blinding and when it would occur and altered their own DNA to pass on protection from the UV light to their offspring. He is trying to use this insignificant fact to prove his ludicrous theory. Deborah personally came to inquire about our process and protocols. She asked me detailed questions about normal octo development and asked for a biopsy of the so-called eyelid tissue. Ludicrous!
END PERSONAL NOTE.

EDIT TO PERSONAL NOTE.

The biopsy confirmed that the muscular tissue is opaque to UV light. The only explanation that makes any sense is that exposure to UV light in ovum altered the DNA of the parent generation, which was passed on to the offspring. The sub-program has been abandoned until further tests can be completed.

NOTES, UNDATED:

AP: Jesus came to see me. We talked for hours, like we used to. He is perfectly lucid, but at times his words seemed delusional. He is convinced that he understands octo intelligence better than ever now. He was deeply troubled, and I am not entirely sure that he's wrong. If the octos have the ability to pass on changes that take place during their lifetimes, it is almost as though they are one continuous mind, passed on forever. Their short lifespan would have no effect on their combined knowledge. However, how do you tell if those changes are chosen? That they are guided by the individual, and not some random process on a cellular level? The implications are great but also limited. The other problem is that we now have very good evidence of their sentience, which means it is ethically unclear how to proceed. We can no longer justify experimentation on the octos, but Jesus kept tossing words like "captivity" around, as though we had to consider the rights of the animals on a level with humans. I cannot imagine such a direction, given how momentous this discovery is. I have decided that we need to continue the observational portion of our program for now.

EXCERPT OF INTERVIEW AUDIO NOTES, SUBJECT DR. J. GALVEZ. DO NOT COPY.

I: Dr. Galvez, are you ready to continue?

JG: Give me a minute. Can you read back what I just said; it's difficult to remember.

I: Certainly. You were explaining the hours leading up to the incident of 12/19, or thereabout. You said that in the days prior, Dr. Alex Piropolous was acting strangely.

JG: Oh, god. Yes. Strangely hardly covers it. It was the Monday before, I believe. I needed Alex to cover my observation shift. The overnights were killing me. So I asked him to cover the nights for a few days. When I came in on Tuesday morning, I couldn't find him to relieve him. I looked all over, and finally found him; he was in the storage closet, in the back of the lab. He appeared to be asleep, but his eyes were open.

I: Was he injured? Unwell in any way?

JG: He didn't appear to be. I mean, he had a strange mark on his collarbone, just below his neck, but it wasn't an injury. Once I woke him and asked about it, he said it had always been there, like a birthmark, but I swear it wasn't. Anyhow, his observations were fastidiously carried out, so I saw no reason to raise the issue with anyone else. I just asked him how he ended up asleep in the closet. He couldn't answer me, and eventually he denied that he'd ever been asleep.

I: What else concerned you?

JG: I recognized something in the way he was acting. It felt familiar—exactly as I felt after my accident with the first brood tank, when I was attacked.

I: Attacked?

JG: I know what the official write-up says, but I was attacked. The largest octopus, the female who had just laid the first batch of eggs, grabbed me around my elbow and bent it back with ferocious strength. I was leaning into the tank, collecting the eggs to move them, and she grew extremely aggressive without warning. She pulled me into the wall of the aquarium and down, so that my watch cracked the glass and my arm shattered it. I was taken to the hospital. I am sure you have reports.

I: I do. I have seen them. How does this relate to what you found on the morning of 12/20?

JG: Alex was acting just like I felt after the attack. I...I don't want this in any official report, you understand. I need to be completely honest with you, but not if I will be quoted.

I: This is a closed investigation. It will never be published.

JG: After my injury, I could hear them, in my head.

I: Them?

JG: The octos. I had a name—I think it's the name they call themselves—in my mind then, but it's gone now. That was why I quit. I couldn't take it. At first, I convinced myself I was hearing things due to the pain meds that the hospital gave me. Then Alex started the UV treatments, and I was overwhelmed by the screaming in my head. I heard their voices, they knew what was happening to them, and they were screaming. Screaming at me, telling me to stop him. I had to leave. It didn't help; I could hear them through the wall. I tried to stop him, but it was too late. I just left.

I: Do you remember what else your delusions included? Did the voices tell you to commit violent acts? Against anyone in particular?

JG: I knew you didn't understand. That's it. Interview over. I want to leave, and if you try to detain me, I will remind you of my rights. I will not be detained against my will.

I: You are free to go, but please do not leave the jurisdiction without contacting my office.

JG: Fuck you.

NOTES, UNDATED, PRESUMED TO COME FROM THE WEEK OF 12/12/19:

AP: I understand now. They have to be freed. This is an impossible situation. The remaining adult ‹unclear› need to be returned to the ocean. They are pleased with what they have learned, but they cannot be allowed to die here. And they will not allow any more to be harmed.

This voice, it is quiet, but I can still hear it, like it's breathing in the back of my head. It is so... so alien. It doesn't even really speak in words. It just puts thoughts in my head. I can see, hear, smell... it. They don't call it the ocean, they don't call it water. But from them, I know it.

Deborah approved all of my supplies, so I just need to wait. They arrive tomorrow. Then I can make a home down here for them. I wish I could tell them what I plan, but I have no way to communicate back to them. So I sit here with them, their menacing voice in my head, filling me with loathing. I can see through their eyes, how alien the world is. But so far, the blind don't speak to me.

‹break of over two hours, where only breathing and background noises are heard.›

I will. I will drive them to the ocean. I am afraid of how they'll react. I need to transport them all in the small tanks. I know you will survive the transport, but I don't know how I'll get you all into the tanks, into the car, down to the dock. I know that you'll understand once you see, but I am afraid of them until I can get them to understand. I mean you no harm! I never did!

LUMINOUS VOLUMES

NOTES, UNDATED, PRESUMED TO IMMEDIATELY FOLLOW THE PREVIOUS ENTRY:

AP: I cannot believe that was successful. I underestimated their ability to catch on to my plan. Once I set up the transport tanks, the larger adults ushered all of the group into them. I barely had to help. I can still feel their voices. It is so dark, and so ancient. It is like having a conversation with a stone. The voice is weathered and old. It is like one voice multiplied, telling me what to do. I tried to tell them over and over as I sat there, there is no way the blind ones can rejoin them. Not in the deep, they will be eaten. I will build it for them, a home. I am building a reef in the basement. It will be large enough for them. It is my doing. It was me who blinded them. I did not know!

‹Indistinct noises›

The mind is so alien, so old. I can see them from inside. They aren't one mind, but many, spread out across eons of memories. Each individual lives its life, but the knowledge is shared and passed on. Each body is nothing more than a neural net, with all of the parts to keep it alive. Like swimming brain that can manipulate its surroundings. I am taking them now. The blind ones will remain here. When I return, I can start on the basement project.

POLICE REPORT, (DATED 12/20/17):

Dr. Alex Piropolous was discovered in a basement of the Aquatic Institute, Building B this morning by Dr. Jesus Galvez. He was taken by emergency services with what appear to be self-inflicted injuries to his eyes. A screwdriver was also found at the scene with what appear to be bloodstains; it was turned over to forensics for testing. It appears that Dr. Piropolous was in the basement for several days prior to being discovered. His wounds are at least several hours old. He was covered in concrete dust and saltwater remnants, most likely from the construction of what Dr. Galvez referred to as an aquarium, though it is much larger than any aquarium I have seen. I didn't see anything alive in there, just dark water behind the glass. Recommend maintaining the perimeter until a complete investigation can take place.

From a brief interview with Dr. Galvez, Dr. Piropolous has not been seen in several days. It is possible that he constructed the basement aquarium alone without anyone's knowledge. Dr. Galvez at first did not realize that Dr. Piropolous was injured, since he was sitting alone in thedark when he was found. Dr. Piropolous was incoherent and I could not interview him at the time. His only words were "Blind. They are not blind." over and over again.

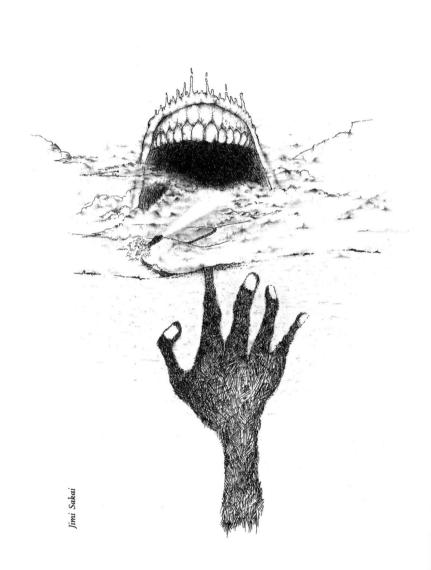

Jimi Sakai

DAVID MᶜCLELLAND

Brendan Ryan's Rocket Car

I wasn't in a position to do anything for Brendan Ryan while he died. The crash threw him out of our rocket car and onto his back, and he lay motionless with his face turned away. The car itself was on top of me, covering me from my chest down. I was trying to keep breathing. The crash scrambled the world. Up and down normalized after a while, but hours and days never did. Somewhere something was on fire, and in the moving firelight Brendan's shoulder was black with blood. Blood was running out of him ceaselessly because his arm was gone below his shoulder. Strips of clouds went strobing by, and beyond them the Big Dipper fell into the pines that edged the field where we had wrecked.

Brendan and I had both been Boy Scouts. To teach us survival skills, or just endurance maybe, the troop leaders had taken us on a camping trip one summer weekend. They hiked us from sunup to sundown and told us to make camp next to a bog, with less equipment than we needed, on gray flats of dried mud. We laid out our bedrolls and at sundown flights of skeeters and midges and no-see-ums came out of the stunted black spruce growing up from the clotted, ebony water and bit at us until dawn. They flew as thick as blizzards of snow and their invisible wings blew tiny breezes onto our eyelids and cheeks and hands as they bit and bit and bit. Out in the oily water something big and black moved and stood up and came toward me. To escape the bloodsuckers Brendan had gone naked into the water and covered himself head to toe with wet black mud and smeared his face until only his eyes and his teeth showed in the moonlight. He told me to come on and do it too and I did and the biting stopped.

Brendan's mother and sister hung a plastic wreath of evergreens and bright forget-me-nots on a white wooden cross planted on the roadside next to where he died. A strange place to find that kind of memorial. Hard to see why anyone would crash here, where the road runs so straight and flat. The ditches to each side are grassy and gently sloped. No one's yet repaired the stone wall we hit, and most likely no one will, because there's no need for a wall there anymore. The stones we knocked back into the field beyond the wall are still marked with the red paint that came off our car and with white scratches where the steel cut through the dirt and moss. The stones are granite, brought up from the permanently chill earth into sun and night and weather, and carefully stacked. They stood for generations until we drove through them.

After he died I dreamt that I explained everything to his mother and sister. In my dream the three of us were in the rocket car that Brendan and I had made, speeding along an endless raceway. I had the pedal screwed to the floor and the engine was ripped open and slamming but we were just barely keeping pace with all the other racing rocket cars. Their tailpipes were afire and their ceramic bodies were so hot with friction that the air peeled off them in ribbons of steam. I pointed at a car that seemed always about to pass us and yet could not.

"Look at it," I said. "Look close."

"It shimmers," Brendan's sister said. "It's splitting. It's like it's turning into two cars. Like it's driving so fast it wants to drive away from itself but it can't."

"Of course not," said Brendan's mother. "We're going at the speed of sound. You can't drive faster than that."

"Yes you can," said his sister.

"I mean the speed of light," his mother said.

"You can't drive faster than yourself," I said. "But that's what Brendan and I were trying to do."

"But you can't," his mother said. "You can't just break all the laws. They wrap around themselves, into a ball, you know. They make up a system."

"Exactly," I said. "That's exactly what Brendan wanted to get outside of, that system. He wanted to look down on all of that from a distance. He wanted to be able to pick it up and hold it in his hand. He wanted to be able to put in his mouth if he wanted to."

"That's ridiculous," his mother said. "We're a part of everything and vicey-versey. We can't escape the system. It's not possible."

"Is it possible?" his sister asked me.

"Think of the mystics who can slow their heartbeats at will," I said. "Or who can change the weather just by closing one eye."

"Nut jobs," his mother said, "is what those people are. What are you saying? That he's somewhere else enjoying all these impossible things all by himself?"

"It's all right here," I said. "He wrote it right here, for you to read."

I pointed to a piece of paper taped to the dashboard. She leaned forward and read, "Dear Mother."

At the wake, after the funeral, only the oldest women talked to me. His great-aunt, and his sister's second-grade teacher. They talked to me out of a sense of social duty, but also I think because I had just been a passenger, and not the driver, so they weren't sure I was not an innocent victim. The scout troop was there too, some in uniform, even the men, and some dressed like everyone else in white shirts and dark jackets and dark ties. They stood in groups, drinking soda, watching me. People speculated that there had been some kind of agreement between me and Brendan. The scouts remembered the time Brendan and I had gone back up the mountain. But there hadn't been any kind of agreement. If I had been the driver there would have been no reason for all these people to be crowding the house. It would have just been me and Brendan eating lunch with his sister and his mother and maybe his sister's friend who was always around. Who today was sitting on the footstool by the cold fireplace with an empty plate on her knees. Watching me.

I tried to appear, not like everything was normal, because of course not, but that I didn't regret being able to be there. That I didn't think I had missed my chance. It should have been easy, because it was true, but with everyone looking at me I didn't know how to act. I thought maybe if I showed an appetite. The food was laid out on a long folding table, and I leaned on my crutches and filled my plate. Egg salad and a red potato salad and another potato salad with bits of pickles. Big bottles of green sodas and different types of cola. Soon the coffee ran out and the empty coffee cups left here and there made it seem as if the wake had already gone on for hours.

The morning of the day after the day we buried him was like any other, except for Brendan's uncle sleeping on the pullout in the living room. I went into the kitchen where his sister was sitting at the card table there and poured her a plastic bowlful of cereal and milk and filled the coffee maker with coffee and water and turned it on. There were crusted casserole dishes in the sink and clean dishes in the drying rack. Tin foil–covered baking pans and lidded soup pots and plastic bowls with plastic tops covered the kitchen counter.

"Tell me about the fast cars," his sister said.

"Tell you what," I said. "What cars, Jenny? Jenny-Jenny. Jennaneena. Jendolyn."

"Stop that," she said. "You and me and my mom in that car. Why were those cars going so fast?"

"They were all Brendan's ideas. Maybe he could explain it.

I can't."

She poked at her cereal with her spoon, turning the colored rings over and over in the pink milk.

She said, "But why were we all in the same dream?"

Her mother came in wearing a bathrobe with the belt tightly tied and the rounded collar turned up around her neck. Her hair was pulled back and her tired face was puffy and uninhabited. She poured herself a cup of coffee and fixed it with skim milk and sweetener from a little pink packet and came to sit at the table. She centered the coffee mug on the placemat in front of her.

"Don't you ever start smoking," she said to her daughter.

"You told me," her daughter said. "You told me and told me."

"Sometimes I want a cigarette so bad," her mother said. "Why can't I have one?"

"Because it's gross."

"What are the other reasons?"

"Because they make people sick. Bad sick."

"Yes," her mother said. "That's why."

She sat and drank her coffee and after a few sips she looked up at me.

"Who made this. You?"

"Yes," I said.

She sat and drank her coffee. In the living room her brother was sleeping on the couch, talking through a dream. She looked at me.

"What?" I said.

She said, "Why are you still here?"

I talked to Brendan's great-aunt Ruth, for a while I think.
I was telling her what kind of car it had been. With the turbo
engine Brendan said we could do 120, 150, 160 on the straight-
aways. If we could have made it to Montana, there's no speed
limit there. Or out on those salt flats. We could outrun the cops,
easy. The cops, Aunt Ruth said. Where were you going to go?
All the way to the Pacific Ocean, I said. All the way to Mexico. A
rocket car. We took the back seat out because we're going to fit
extra tanks in there. A second fuel tank and a tank for what's it
called—methane—and one for water for the carburetor. So we
can drive for days without filling up. I stopped talking when I
realized she had stopped answering. The rocket car was scrap.
Sergeant Orville told Brendan's mother he could see the car was
illegal in umpteen different ways before they even put out the
engine fire. Brendan's mother told Sergeant Orville to break
it apart into little tiny bits and bury them, please. It does look
like the boys put some work into it, he said. Please, she told him.

I took Aunt Ruth's paper plate and empty cup from her.

"Let me get these," I said.

I went away to the kitchen, but Uncle Bill who had the salvage
yard and Brendan's other uncle and the town librarian and more
people I didn't look in the face to know exactly who-all it was
all stopped talking and moved away from me, as if out of polite-
ness. I folded Aunt Ruth's plate into a semicircle and flattened
her paper cup and carefully slotted them both into the already
overstuffed garbage can and everyone in the kitchen watched
as if just to make sure this was properly done. I nodded to the
room and they mumbled back at me and I went out and down
the hallway to see what Brendan was doing.

I opened the door to his room and the room was cool inside and he was not there. He had left his bed unmade. Someone had drawn the window shade and pulled the blue curtains closed, and then, almost as if I had really forgotten, I remembered that he was dead.

On the wall was the poster of Larry Bird wearing his mustache and his green jersey and spinning a basketball on one finger. Books were stacked on the little desk and the floor and overfilled the bookshelves, all of them bookmarked with scraps of torn paper. Most were from the town library, and I knew they had already been overdue before the accident. The librarian had asked Brendan to do him a favor and release just a few hostages before he'd let him take out anything else.

Brendan said, "Okay, Mr. Thicket. I won't need them forever."

The librarian was looking at a list of titles on the computer monitor in front of him.

He said, "What if someone wants to learn about the Egyptians burying their dead. Or the Native Americans burying their dead. Or wants a book on cars or airplanes or engines or rocketry. Or the German aircraft of World War Two. Or the history of flight in general. Or wants to read something by Mr. D. T. Suzuki. Anything by Mr. Suzuki. Because looks like you've got it all."

"Okay, Mr. Thicket," Brendan said.

"And you too," the librarian said to me. "You boys share some interests. Electricity. Spiritualism, mesmerism. The Rosicrucians. Witchcraft. Combustion engines. NASA. Reincarnation. If you could just return a small percentage. A book by each author. Or maybe one from each subject."

"Okay, Mr. Thicket," I said.

Taped on the walls of Brendan's room were pictures of American and German bombers and F-1 Tomcats and the Batmobile and the General Lee and diagrams of car engines and plane engines. There were other diagrams, too, diagrams Brendan had made in colored pen of arrows pointing into and out of triangles and concentric circles. Some triangles were doubled and some were tripled, their corners misaligned and the distances between them marked in degrees. The pen lines were ruler-straight and the center points of the compass-drawn circles were punched through the paper. There was math on these diagrams. Calculations of force, trajectory and velocity. There were ornate symbols he had copied out of library books. At the center of a grouping of circles pierced by several lines was the infinity sign, the double loop.

Also taped among the diagrams was a handwritten page. Written and signed and recently dated by Brendan and addressed to his mother. I read it. I took it off the wall and folded it and put it in my pocket.

The troop leaders took us on an overnight up into the mountains one spring. We broke camp and started hiking down in the early morning. It was cold, but the hiking warmed us. There was a Pathfinder at the head of the line to read the blazes, and an old man who was let out of carrying even his own pack walked with a stick at the end of the line, but the spaces between the scouts stretched as the hike went on and soon Brendan and I were walking silently alone through the pines. A runoff stream crossed the trail back and forth and pooled in the foot-worn gullies. White quartz sparkled in the wet rocks.

We went off the trail through a cut in the trees and followed a narrow path of bare dirt twisting through high bushes and saplings. The bushes gave way to sheer empty air and we stood on a shallow outcrop of rock and looked down the mountainside into the black and green treetops. Far below and out away from the foot of the mountain a turkey vulture tipped and swung above a curve of road, and beyond that was a vast floor of trees dappled black by cloud shadows, and then the hills at the horizon. White clouds shifted in great sheets through the blue air.

When we came back to the trail the last of the line was just walking out of sight. He had tied a red bandana around his white-haired head. We stood quietly to let him go. The entire troop and the troop leaders had moved down the trail ahead of us. We turned and went back up the mountain. When they came for us, just a few men, it was late evening. Too dark to hike out.

Brendan's Uncle Bill had made an awning of corrugated metal that attached on one side to the back of the Ryans' house. He had meant it to be a sunshade for picnic lunches in hot weather but instead we kept our car there. The car was a black '61 Oldsmobile F85 and we had winched out the 215 engine and dropped in a Jetfire Turbo from a '63 Jetfire that had been trucked into Uncle Bill's yard with both axles broken. We made mistakes for months before we installed the Jetfire

Turbo correctly. The weight of the engine drove the nose of the car down and the tail rose up to show the tops of the tires and where the shocks attached to the body. We used an acetylene torch to cut away the glove box and the dead radio and almost the entire dashboard to give us access to the engine from inside the car. The F85 lacked for seats both front and back and we used the torch to braze in two bucket seats with ripped cushions. The floor on the passenger's side was rusted away to an open hole and we dropped a shaft of rebar across it to make a footrest.

"Needs new tires," Brendan said. "These are bare. See the mesh?"

"We're going to do all the George Barris things later," I said. "We can switch them then."

"But still we could test it," he said. "Right now."

Brendan sat in the driver's seat with the door open and one foot out on the grass and as he revved the engine the right front of the car lifted. As if the engine might torque high enough to shear off its bolts and flip out of the car and into the grass. He looked at me.

"Why not?" he said. "As good a day as any."

The accident splintered bones in my foot and I had a cast from my toes to my knee with a bent piece of steel coming out of the heel for me to walk on. At Christmas Brendan's mother had cooked a roast and carved it at the table, the round brown end of the bone sticking out of the wet red wall of meat. The doctor said I would heal fine. He said we should keep an eye on my knee for future cartilage damage, it might rip—the cartilage—later on, possibly, let's keep an eye on it. But I walked out of the hospital. With just the cast and the crutches.

I stood for a while looking around Brendan's room.

One time after school we wedged rolled towels at the head and foot of the closed door and smoked bowl after bowl of weed. We thought Brendan's mom was working both the afternoon and the late shift. We had tried a few of the spells Brendan had been collecting and now we were goofing around with Larry Bird in the poster on the wall, and he was so high from our smoke he couldn't say his own name.

"Barry Lird," he said. "Barry Lird. Mr Lird."

He had the basketball spinning on a fingertip and in his other hand he had a brass nameplate, like you might see on a banker's desk, that said Mr. B. Lird. We were doubled up laughing with our hands on our hurting bellies and our faces cut open into gigantic smiles. I could feel my mouth going dry from having been open for so long. The muscles in my abdomen were completely seized, like the pistons of an overheated engine.

We heard the car pull up outside and the front door open and Larry straightened up and stopped laughing and said we'd better go, and we pulled the towels and went out the window. By the time Brendan's mother had put her purse and a bag of groceries on the kitchen counter and come out back to tell us that she was off early and making chicken breasts for dinner we were standing under the metal awning chewing Bubblicious and pointing out the Olds's empty engine mount to each other.

I began pulling the library books from the shelves and stacking them in piles on the floor. Brendan's sister came to the open door and watched me for a moment and went away and came back with her mother. There were other people, too, looking in.

"What are you doing?" her mother said.

"They're library books," I said. "They're my library books. I'm going to return them."

She put her hand to her face and turned and went through the people clustering the hallway behind her. Mr. Thicket stood in the doorway and looked in. He made "come here" motions at me, like someone standing on the shore waving a swimmer in from deep waters.

"Just leave those be," he said. "Leave them. We'll worry about that later. Now is not the time for this. Come out of there."

"You'd better," Larry Bird said.

"Come out of there," Mr. Thicket said.

I looked at the window but the shade was still down and the curtains were still closed. Larry Bird shook his head, like, don't do it. I went out of the room and Mr. Thicket put his hand on my shoulder and walked me down the short hallway past a double row of people standing up against the photos on the walls, holding their drinks and their plates at chest level out of my way. He walked me to the living room where the food on the long table was undiminished for all that people had been eating steadily all morning and he released me into the center of the room.

With Brendan's mom in her bedroom and most of the people now looking into Brendan's room as if at a re-creation of the crash itself, the living room was nearly empty. Aunt Ruth saw me standing there and seemed to firm up somehow and ready herself for me. I could see her doing this, getting ready for whatever conversation I might impose upon her, and the thought of being the person for whom that kind of preparation was necessary was so awful that I went through the kitchen and out the back. I held the screen door as it closed to keep it from slamming and rattling the decorative plates that hung on the kitchen walls in their wire holders.

Heavy weather had come on suddenly since the burial. The snow on the ground was squirrel-tracked and some larger animal passing through had splashed a wide furrow across the yard. The metal awning was glassy with ice and underneath it the snow was wind-drifted and shallow and showed the black dirt where the oil pan and the fuel lines and the coolant had all spilled again and again. The red tool box was open, its three drawers stepped out and its lid up, and the top drawer was filled with snow like a frosted cake in a cake pan. Embossed in the surface of the snow were the shapes of our scattered tools, tools Uncle Bill had lent us. Old tools. I began collecting them, running my hands through the snow. Some of them were rusted solid and didn't work at all, like models of a tool we might have needed, made to scale but useless.

Ryan's sister came out of the kitchen door and let it bang shut behind her.

"What are you doing?" she asked me.

"Getting these tools together," I said.

"Are they yours?"

"No. Uncle Bill's mostly."

"Why are you out here all alone?"

"I'm not all alone. Aren't you out here with me?"

"Before I came out you were all alone."

SKRYPTOR

"Listen. Jennybaby. Why don't you go in with your mom."

"She's in her bedroom crying right now. Are those Brendan's tools?"

"No. They're Uncle Bill's tools."

"What are you going to do with them?"

"Return them, I guess. Sometime."

"Do you think he's coming back?"

"Did he leave? Uncle Bill?"

"My brother."

"Coming back?"

"Yes," she said.

She was young. She didn't understand, and no one had explained anything to her.

"Oh, no. Do I think he's coming back? No."

"So it's all right to take his stuff."

"Those were my books," I said. "I took those books out of the library under my own name."

She stood on the block of concrete that served for a back step with her shiny black shoes, looking past the yard's broken fence at the grove of linden trees that leaned in toward each other as if they were talking and saying just how tired they were. The sky at the funeral had been gray and it continued that way above us now. Her friend came to the kitchen door in her black dress and looked out at us.

"You know," I said, "in some ways it's like he didn't really leave."

"What do you mean?"

"I mean if we remember him, it's like he's not really gone."

She said, "If he's not gone, why do we need to remember him?"

She turned and went back in the house and her friend looked

through the screen door at me and I made a face at her and she went away and I went back to gathering the tools out of the snow and the oily dirt, but when I had them together they were more than I could carry. I dropped them in a pile and left.

I took the tools to Uncle Bill in a pair of doubled-up black plastic bags. I walked down the highway outside the guardrail like a trash picker. The salvage-yard gates were chained and locked, so I threw the tools over and climbed the fence where Brendan had folded the top twists of sharpened wire flat. My foot didn't hurt much anymore. I walked down the shadowed rows of abundant wreckage. Around me metal ticked as the morning warmed. A line of unbroken windshields was stacked against each other on the ground, the daylight falling through their green depths and into the shifting blackness at the end of that glass tunnel. I didn't expect Uncle Bill to be in the trailer that he used as an office but I knocked anyway and was surprised to hear him say, "What."

I opened the door and he was at his desk with the day's paper and a cup of coffee. The small room smelled of coffee and dusty paper and dead cigarettes. The orange wires of an electric heater burned by his feet.

"Jesus fucking Christ," he said. "You're lucky Blackie's dead. He would have taken your leg off."

"I'm just bringing these back."

I held up the clanking black bags.

"What the hell is that," he said.

I set the bags on the floor and took out the tools. He stood up with his hands flat on his desk and leaned to look at them laid out in the dirt of the filthy floor tiles.

"I really gave you boys a shit selection," he said. "Didn't I."

I held up a socket wrench we had discovered to be metric.

"We soaked it in oil like you said but it still won't turn. I thought you would want them back."

He sat down.

"No, I don't want them back. I mean, goddamn it, you can leave them. But I don't want them. These are what you used to build that piece of shit aren't they."

"Yes.

"Where's that toolbox, though. I thought I gave you a pretty good toolbox."

I started to tell him that the drawers had rusted open and the plastic handle had come off the lid but he interrupted.

"Forget it. That toolbox was a piece of shit too. I don't believe you got that engine in."

"Well, we got it in."

"I never thought you'd get it in. I never thought you'd get it running."

"Well, we got it running."

"This is the worst thing that ever happened to her," he said. "Her husband was bad enough. That asshole. But hey, we're all adults. But this I don't know if she'll ever really come back from. Because why should she? And you. Don't you think he meant to take you with him?"

"I don't know."

"You don't know. Well, you're the only one who doesn't know."

He sat with his hands flat on his desk and looked at me.

"You didn't think I'd be here is the only reason you came this early," he said. "You've got to stop sneaking around like this. Go live your own life. While you still got it."

When I got back to the house Brendan's mother asked me in to the kitchen and we sat at the table there.

"I saw you," she said. "You were sitting out on the back fence when the sun rose. Then you came and got up all those things from the yard."

"I'm sorry. I thought you'd all be sleeping."

"No. Around dawn I'm awake pretty much every day now. I wake up in the dark and I'm just exhausted. I lie there and after a while the light comes up. Then I give up on sleeping and come out to the kitchen. It's a weird thing. It's like going underwater to a shipwreck of my own kitchen. Like those divers that find shipwrecks and go through them for treasure and history and whatnot."

"Yes," I said.

She sat with one hand smoothing the flat white tablecloth.

"You have to give us a break for a while," she said. "It's bothering to Jenny. You have to just let us be for a little bit. Not come around."

"Because of why. Because of Jenny?"

"No. Because of you. Because you're already a year older than he'll ever be. And the older we see you get the farther away he goes."

"I'm sorry," I said.

"Of course you are," she said. "We're all sorry."

On the way out of the salvage yard Brendan and I stopped

at the circle of cut-up dirt where Uncle Bill kept Blackie chained to a post. The tops of his ears had been chewed ragged when he was a pup but those other dogs were gone now and he was still standing. There was gray along his thin black lips and salting his coat. His eyes were black in their bony gray sockets. His tail was a stub and the fur above his shoulders was rough and scarred as if he had been born with improbable dog wings that had also been docked, down to their sockets. But he was still firmly muscled and at his full weight and stood straight without the restless shifting that betrays an older dog. Immobile at the end of his coiled chain.

"Don't do it," I said. "Let's just go."

"Don't what," Brendan said.

He stood outside the dirt circle and looked at the dog and the dog stood and looked back at us. His dry black nose working as he read the air going by him. The smells of metal and rust and the cold, wet dirt of the yard.

"Let him be."

"I'm not bothering him. He just stands tied to that post all day."

"Uncle Bill says he lets him loose."

"He just lets him out on the rats. Saves on dog food."

Brendan took a step and the dog watched his feet as they crossed the line and then raised his head to look up at Brendan now standing inside the circle and then looked back to Brendan's feet. Utterly self-contained in his watchfulness. Not shifting his paws or twitching the rigid nub of his tail. Just looking at Brendan and at his empty hands and then at me to see what I would do.

LUMINOUS VOLUMES

"It's all right," Brendan said.

The dog looked up at him.

"He'll jump," I said. "You know he will."

Brendan said, "It's all right, old dog. Not much longer."

I thought if I stepped inside the circle I would be able to distract the dog from anything Brendan might do, so I stepped forward and the dog turned his head just slightly to watch me. We stood there for some time and the dog never moved from watching us. A mourning dove called from beyond the fence and one of the dog's ears swiveled back to listen and then came forward again and we three stood there.

Brendan touched my shoulder and we stepped backward together.

We turned our backs to the dog and went past the rows of cars lying on their bellies in the dirt and the tilted stacks of rotten wooden fencing and past towers of broken bricks taller than ourselves. I heard the chain move and looked back and the dog was at the edge of the circle watching us go. Never having barked or growled or made any sound at all except for the chain clicking on itself as it pulled through the dust.

I sat on the back fence and watched the house. There were night sounds in the trees behind me. Raccoons went humping across the wide lawns from the garbage cans by the Ryans' garage to the neighboring houses. Toward dawn birds began flying. At first they were not even shaped into birds. They were just movements in the dark at the rooftops, and then as they began singing I could follow them in flight from tree to roofline and back. The dawn came up light as mist, as if it might evaporate and disappear like mist, and there was a time when the birds were still and the birdsong paused, and then the sun rose and it was morning.

The house lay on its lot, the white siding chalky with dew, and the windows dark. Single story and nearly flat-roofed. Brendan's was the only curtained window. The rusted awning where we had made our auto shop sheltered nothing but the brown wet grass that stretched in the cold fall morning across all the long spaces between the few houses on the street. There were black and brown birds flying, crows and starlings and greased-up grackles. I watched the kitchen window but I didn't see Brendan's mother there.

I went back to our house. There were dishes in the sink and a lacquer of coffee browning the glass coffee pot and the top of the kitchen table was smeary. A stack of pizza boxes leaned on an overfilled garbage can with trash overflowing onto the floor around it. My sister's shoes were just where she had dropped them when she packed to leave, scattered in a continuous line from her bedroom down the hall and through the kitchen to the door. High heels and flats and sneakers. For different occasions, she had said when she bought them. But they were all of them just five-dollar shoes and now they all looked the same, kicked across the floor, cheap and dirty and left behind.

The living room was the same as it had been five years ago when I first met Brendan Ryan. A low coffee table matched the heavy wood-framed couch and the wicker-backed armchairs. A braided oval rug lay on the tan carpet. We had been in the house for less than a month before my mother's funeral. Brendan saw all the cars parked in front of the house and the somber people in dark clothes and walked into the house as confident as if he had a job to do and came right up to talk to me. Because we were the same age about, he told me. And because his father was gone too, but not his mother, at least not yet. Tall brass floor lamps. A television and a stereo system in matching cabinets. All of it unplugged. To save on electricity, my sister said. But by now the electricity had been off for months.

I went in and sat on the couch. Five years ago my father had left, and two years ago my mother had moved us to this house and almost immediately been killed by a bus as she drove to her new job, and a year ago last spring Brendan and I had built the rocket car. And then we took it out on the straight safe road and Brendan drove at such a speed that when he jerked the wheel over we cleared the drainage ditch—front and back tires both—before we hit the wall.

I was tired from having been up so early to watch the Ryan house and I let myself fall asleep on the couch. Dust. Old smoke. Sunlight the color of dirty brown river water. Hours and days and months and years pressed into the fabric of that couch. I woke up panicky, having heard someone calling to me, telling me to come on. I thought maybe my sister was angry at me for sleeping on the couch with my coat and shoes on, but I stood up and, no, she still hadn't come back. And the voice I had heard wasn't hers anyway.

DAVID M^cCLELLAND

LUMINOUS VOLUMES

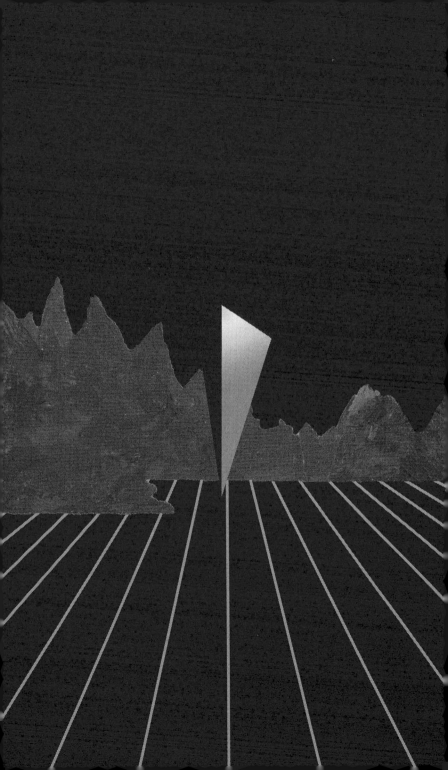

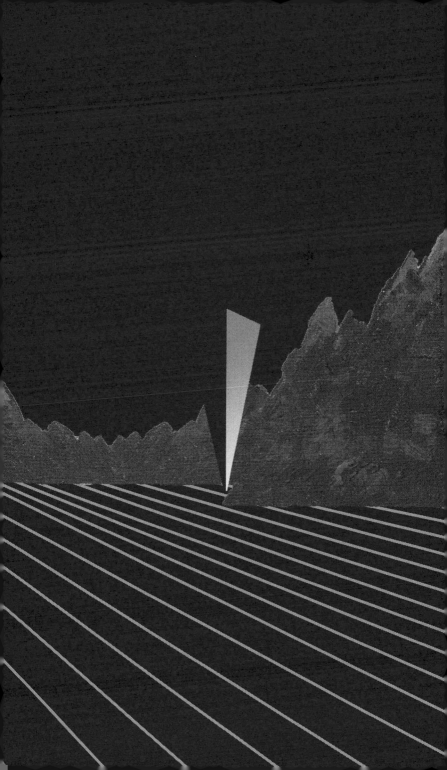

"BRIGHTS"   RHALLIS

Rich Hall

Brights

Officer O'Malley responded to the call. He was only a mile away and was already headed in that direction. No word yet on what happened to the line, just that it was hanging low across Highway 12. "Slumping," is how the caller described it.

Sure enough. It was slumping. At its lowest, the power line was less than ten or twelve feet from the asphalt. O'Malley pulled onto the shoulder and turned on his overhead lights. He shifted into park but left the car running.

"Dispatch, any word on when MPC's plannin' on gettin' here?" O'Malley settled into his seat and glanced around the car for a Coke.

"They're hoping to get there in under an hour," dispatch reported.

"Roger. Thanks."

An hour? Jesus. Probably the wind. Montana Power Company was repairing lines all over town, but they should know this one is a priority. Can't have a line drooping over a state highway.

This gave O'Malley time to catch up on paperwork—the glamorous part of law enforcement. Occasionally a car would approach and he'd glance up to make sure they were low enough to limbo under the line. Lucky this happened after folks had already gotten home from work. O'Malley's mind wandered.

Was Officer Martinez hitting on him earlier today? O'Malley had been sending her signals since she joined the highway patrol a few weeks ago, but she hadn't reciprocated. Until earlier today during roll call.

"So, are Fridays show-'n-tell now?" Martinez had said, pointing to O'Malley's Zippo. "How about you show tonight at the Tar Bar and I'll tell?"

"Oooo, smooth Officer, maybe I will." And was that a wink?

A truck towing a horse trailer approached O'Malley's squad car from behind. O'Malley stepped out and motioned for the truck to stop.

"Evenin', Officer, everything all right?"

"Yeah, we just got a low line up ahead there. You know your clearance?"

"Shouldn't be more than seven feet." The man nudged his hat back with his knuckle. "Think I can make it?"

"Let's have ya pull onto the shoulder as you go under. You'll be fine there."

And he was. He waved as he drove off. Into the sunset, as it were. O'Malley checked his watch. Near eight. It's been more than an hour. Where the hell were those guys?

He was running low on gas, so he turned his car off. He didn't want to drain the battery, so he killed the overhead lights a few minutes later. He'd put out some flares instead. O'Malley popped his trunk then realized he'd forgotten to grab more this morning. Last night he used the last of them directing traffic around a rollover on I-90. He let the trunk lid fall shut.

Back to paperwork. Back to daydreaming. Evening dreaming. Martinez's smile was definitely genuine. She was finally opening up. But did she say she'd be at the Tar Bar for sure? O'Malley texted her. "So, Tar Bar tonight?"

She didn't text back right away. Of course not. Why would she? She's on the clock just like he was. He knew that. She was probably driving. Or breaking up some domestic disturbance back in town. Plus, even if she were sitting on the side of the road somewhere, she still wouldn't text back right away. That would make her seem desperate. Like she'd been waiting for him to text her. O'Malley was young enough to know how these games were played. If anything, he may have been a bit too forward in his text. He had only texted her once before. It was one of those, "Yeah, we should grab lunch sometime, I'll tell you about the force, let me get your number," conversations. O'Malley's text had been: "This is Paul." Martinez had just smiled and said "great, thanks," but she didn't respond to the text.

O'Malley looked at his phone. Still no response from Martinez. He unlocked it and looked at their message history. Just his two texts. No response.

Night had now wrestled control away from the evening. O'Malley asked dispatch about where the power company was, and was told that they were on their way. Fifteen minutes, they said, max.

O'Malley turned on his squad car's spotlight and shined it up at the line. It swayed in the wind, but didn't make a noise. No buzzing. No sparks. Just a sway. Like a hammock on a lazy afternoon.

Sapling was running late. He hadn't been through this part of Montana before and was questioning whether Google Maps had led him astray.

The other drivers call him "Sapling" because he's young and new to the company. He'd driven for Savage Trucking since right after high school, but he was new to Godfrey. On his first haul another driver asked his name over the CB. Sapling said "Ya'll can call me Redwood, like the tree." Except when he said it, his voice cracked. From that day forward they called him Sapling. He'd even come to think of himself as Sapling.

He lifted the microphone of his CB and said, "Raybands, you still there?"

"Yup, this is Raybands," a gruff voice crackled through the radio, "how ya doin', Sapling? You on the backstroke?"

"Negative, not yet. I'm still outside of Missoula."

There was a static pause, then, "Well what's goin' on? What's got ya runnin' so far behind?"

"Google has me on some back road, ya know Highway 12?" Sapling asked.

"Yeah, I know it. What's yur twenty?"

"Eastbound on the 12, just crossed the state line. If I stay on the 12 will it run me right into Missoula?"

"Ain'tcha got yur maps, Sapling? The real ones, made a laminated paper?"

"Yeah, I got 'em, but I don't have time to be inspectin' 'em on the side a the damn highway."

"Well, greenhorn, the 12 is gonna run ya into a lil' chicken shit town called Lolo...come to think of it, I think Rumble Weed is from Lolo. Hmm, anyway, when ya get to Lolo, head north on 93. That'll take ya right up Missoula's ass."

"I 'preciate it, Raybands."

"Think ya can manage from there?"

"That oughta do it."

"Alrighty, young buck, see ya Sunday."

A few drivers were planning on meeting up at a Love's in Idaho Falls for a convoy heading east. They'd meet up at the truck stop, share stories and lot lizards, then head out first thing Monday morning.

Sapling was supposed to be in a bar at this time of night. Whiskey and Coke. Cigarettes. Maybe some tail, if the locals were amiable. He cursed Google Maps for the thirteenth time. Sapling wasn't the kind of driver who loved to drive. This wasn't fun for him. He did it because he needed money. He had child support to pay, and this was the only way he could pay it. This was a job, and when a job that was supposed to be wrapped up around four in the afternoon still wasn't over by 8:00 p.m., Sapling took it personal.

Flush with frustration, Sapling told Siri to "Pay Seek & Destroy, by Metallica" and cranked it up. He put the hammer down and flooded his Peterbilt engine with diesel. He pushed his truck to the edge, then held it there. He checked his mirrors, half expecting his load of Dodge Rams to roll off the trailer. The wind didn't help, but it had mostly died down. Like a ship at sea roughing a tempest, he swayed to the waves of Highway 12.

Alex was totally gonna be pissed.

Amanda texted her, "IMS, just left, Emma's a total bitch. ILBL8,"

Amanda was right, Alex was pissed, "WTF Amanda?"

"Emma wouldn't give me the keys. OMW." Amanda set her phone in her lap and clicked through the radio presets to find something other than commercials for online "universities." Emma really had been a total bitch. She had promised Amanda that Amanda could use her car tonight, then changed her mind at the last second. Amanda had promised to give Alex a ride to a bonfire tonight where Alex planned to finally hook up with Benny Carter.

Amanda had to beg her mom to borrow the Bronco. Her mom had given her shit about it because two months ago she sideswiped a parked car. But it's not like the Bronco was even that damaged. It had, like, a tiny scrape down the side that insurance paid for anyway. Really, her mom should thank her for the insurance money.

"Whatever, just hurry. Started like an hour ago," Alex texted.

Amanda knew that. The party started at dusk. Amanda

SKRYPTOR

didn't consider herself to be that popular, but she totally was. Her eyes were big and spaced perfectly, her nose was small and smooth, and when she smiled, her thin lips exposed only her bright-white orthodontically straight teeth (no gums). Her boyishly square jaw worked with her platinum blonde pixie cut to frame her face like a freshly finished Michelangelo masterpiece. Plus, her skin was as pure and smooth as milk. As a result of her cosmetic perfection, Amanda was a lightning rod for the envious bitches in her class.

She texted Colby, "U gonna be there tnite?"

He texted back right away, "Already here. U coming?"

"Only if u make me." She knew Colby would get it. Ever since homecoming she and Colby had been sneaking out together. They usually climbed onto a roof downtown and made out for hours. Two nights ago Amanda went down on Colby for the first time. He didn't last long. Then, last night, Colby went down on her. She didn't last long either, but her quick recharge kept Colby busy until dawn's early light.

Tonight she would lose her virginity. She just knew it. All day she had been thinking about it. Her fantasies made her stomach fizz like a shaken Coke.

"U no Ill make u. RSN," Colby texted. Amanda couldn't take her eyes of the text. She read it over and over. Then a car behind her honked. She looked up and saw that the light had turned green, so she flipped off the car behind her and kept driving. She was a pro at texting and driving. The trick was to hold the phone at the top of the steering wheel so you could see the screen and the road at the same time. She thought of something clever to say to Colby as her Bronco drifted down the road, bouncing from the white shoulder line to the yellow centerline like a child-thrown bowling ball down a lane with the bumpers up.

Sapling whipped his rig around corner after corner, hoping that Lolo was hiding behind one of them. The sky had turned blacker than rubber, so he hit the brights. Highway 12 was flanked by forest. Thick pines lined the winding road just behind the guardrails. A smartass sign told him that the road curved up ahead and to slow it down to forty-five miles per hour. Which meant sixty was safe.

As he rounded one of the corners, his brights lit up a cop car on the opposite shoulder. Fuckin' County Mountie, probably pointing a speed gun at him. He downshifted and braced for the explosion of blue and red from the roof of the squad car. It would flip a U-turn and tuck its hood under the back of Sapling's trailer.

Instead, the officer was standing in the road waving a flashlight back and forth, like he needed help.

Sapling stood on the brake pedal and brought the complaining semi to a screeching, bumping, jangling stop.

When the truck settled back and the air brakes let out their sighs, the officer walked across the road toward Sapling's door. Sapling rolled his window down and looked down at the officer.

"Jesus Christ, let me guess, bees?" Officer O'Malley asked.

"Nah, no. Just runnin' behind." Sapling said, as ashamed as he could make it.

"Well, the speed limit through these corners is forty-five miles per hour, ya best stick to it."

"Will do, Officer, sorry for the trouble." Sapling put his

truck into gear and let off the brake when Officer O'Malley stopped him.

"Woah, woah, hold up. There's a slumping power line here." He pointed his flashlight up ahead and Sapling saw the line. A thin black cable just above eye level. There was no way he'd fit under that. Another goddamn delay. Officer O'Malley turned back to Sapling and asked, "You don't have any flares on ya, do ya? 'Fraid I'm out."

Sapling said, "Sure thing, one sec," and unbuckled his seat-belt. He turned on his hazards, lifted his armrest and walked to the back of his cab. He found his flare pack next to his extra toilet paper. He heard a thump outside and thought Officer O'Malley had banged on his door.

"On my way," Sapling said. "I'm hurryin'."

Amanda was texting Emma. Emma needed to know that being bitchy was not cool. Emma was jealous so she tried to sabotage Amanda's night.

She rounded a corner on Highway 12—a road she had been driving her entire life and could probably drive blindfolded—and was nearly blinded by some jackass who hadn't turned off his brights. She checked to make sure she was in her lane then continued her text: "Is this cause of Colby? U no I didnt steal him. He—"

The thump-crash of a deer's body hitting the Bronco's bumper then windshield was loud enough to scare Amanda into hysterics. She screamed and buried the brake pedal. The

Bronco slid to a stop. She was shaking and hardly breathing. Just enough for a slight sob, a quiver. Her eyes darted into the night through her crushed windshield and couldn't see anything. She looked in her rearview mirror and saw a semi-truck's tail lights and blinking hazards. The jackass that hadn't turned off his brights. Her phone was on the dashboard up against the broken windshield. Hands trembling, she retrieved her phone and opened her door.

She stepped out slowly. Sometimes the deer isn't dead. She looked at her phone; she had to call the cops. Her screen was shattered and the display was glitching. She looked back at the truck, silently parked in the middle of its lane. Did it hit the deer first? Or another deer from the herd? Amanda stepped around her door and looked in front of her car.

Several yards away, lit by the Bronco's perdiddle, Officer O'Malley's lifeless body punctuated a bloody exclamation point streaked into the road.

Schlachthausvision

A.

B.

Fig. 1.

Paul Nitsche

Slaughterhouse Vision

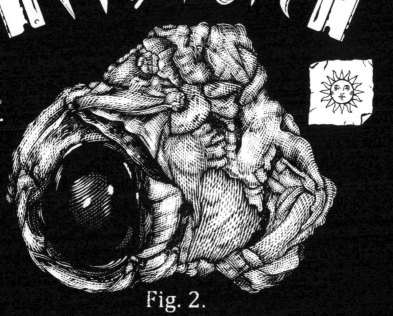

Fig. 2.

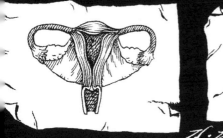

MARIA GABRIELE BAHER
Slaughterhouse Vision

The professor waits at the backdoor of the slaughterhouse. The air is thick with morning fog. That's the way it is in Vienna and around slaughterhouses. Fog, always fog. Who has ever seen a slaughterhouse in a gentle breeze and sunshine? No one. He certainly never has. And he has come here every November since 1998. Schlachthof Zehn, Slaughterhouse Ten. The cobblestone-covered alley, the heavy gray metal doors, the tracks under the roof's overhang holding hooks that carry cows' halves into the hollow of delivery trucks, the gut-smeared loading dock, the blood-brown puddles, the opaque seepage between the stones— all of it—it is not his turf. His turf is a sparse top-floor studio in a more manicured section of town, nightly dinners of cold cuts and sliced bread, and a wall of books relevant to his métier.

He only comes to the slaughterhouse for his yearly bag of eyeballs. Bulls' eyes including sockets. He stands, awkwardly hunched, by the massive backdoor, his horn-rimmed glasses barely balancing on the tip of his nose, his well-worn fedora pulled over his thinning hair, and a proper Burberry trench coat hiding his expanded middle. He, E. (period) A. (period) Lugerbauer, is a Professor of Biology at an extremely well-respected high school. He believes in a hands-on approach to teaching. He has made a point (and a reputation) of providing his students with bulls' eyes, which they will dissect using razor blades. Under his supervision, of course. Nothing explains the miracle of vision like peeling back the layers of an eyeball, pulling the iris from between cornea and lens, then separating the optic nerve and pointing out the blind spot. The students love it. And perhaps they momentarily love him. Who else would let them handle razor blades and eyeballs?

E. A. Lugerbauer knows how to acquire high-quality eyeballs. He has a connection: Jack the butcher. Perhaps the man's name isn't really Jack. But who has ever seen a butcher named Sebastian or Humphrey or even Edgar Adam? No one. So, it's Jack the Butcher. Yesterday the Professor and Jack traded messages confirming the pickup of "a dozen bulls' and/or cows' eyes, plenty of muscle and nerve attached, fresh." It is of utmost importance to receive eyeballs fresh and to use them for same-day dissection. Once, the Professor had to keep the dozen eyeballs in his fridge overnight because a school wide unannounced fire-drill had preempted his class. The eyes sat like dark, faceless pocket watches in a Tupperware container wedged between leftover rice salad and assorted cold cuts. The dissection two days later was less joyful.

The Professor pounds on the gray metal slaughterhouse door. Three times. He expects Jack with bloody apron and bearded smile to open the heavy door and to pass him the eye-bag in exchange for the usual carton of Pall Mall. The eyeballs are a bargain. This time, though, the door stays closed. No steps approach, no hinges move. He pounds again. Jack might be busy? Butchering? Using the WC? The Professor waits a few more moments, then he turns up and stiffens the collar of his coat. He pounds again, with more heft, and suddenly he feels as if he is impersonating Harry Lime from The Third Man on a mission in WWII-ravaged Vienna, which still looks war-ravaged right here, in the back alley of this slaughterhouse.

Finally, the door opens. It's not Jack. It's a small sturdy woman, maybe in her middle fifties, wearing a thick, properly blood-smeared apron and holding a large knife. The handles of two smaller knives stick from a pocket of her apron. Who's ever seen a lady butcher? No one. Until now.

"Yeah?" She throws a grunt at him. She looks positively bothered, as if all the cow carcasses behind her were very interesting guests she has been forced to abandon in the midst of a deftly entertaining private soiree.

"Uhh...excuse me, Fräulein?" says E.A.L.

She huffs immediately, a slicing sort of huff that clarifies her distaste for flattery. "What," she goes on. It isn't a question. "What's with the banging!"

"I am here... I have a... this is my..." E.A. Lugerbauer stammers. He doesn't do well when things don't go according to plan in places that are not his turf. He doesn't do well when facing a butcheress wielding—perhaps not really wielding, but certainly brandishing—a knife.

"Is Jack available?" he finally manages, dry-throated.

"JACK," she has a cutting tone when she says the name,

"JACK got fired. It's me now." With that she wants to leave him and return to her beef sides. She moves to close the door, but E.A.L., in a surprising display of physical impulse, wedges his leg into the doorframe. He will not disappoint his students! He will not forgo the one moment of his students' affection, the single most precious reward he is granted in exchange for the eyeballs.

"Ah Christ..." she sighs as she stops short of amputating his leg. "Whaaaat else...?" She opens the door again. He pulls his leg back.

"Would you... I came by... the reason..." He doesn't quite know how to go on.

"Spit it out, Harry Lime!" she says. Ah! So it's not just him making the Third Man connection. There is something Harry Lime-ish about him. Must be the trench coat. If he were Harry Lime he wouldn't stutter, if he were Harry Lime, even for a moment, he would command...

"I am here for my one dozen eyeballs." There, he said it. Commanding.

"Your dozen eyeballs?? Did I hear you right? You are at my door asking for your dozen eyeballs?" She juts her face forward. It's quite a face. Raw-red cheeks. Moss-green eyes. Good lips, like pork strips, plump and fleshy... An awful and stunning face. The Butcher Frau from Schlachthof Zehn.

"I have a longstanding arrangement with Jack. He supplies me with—"

"Jack got fired. Didn't I already say Jack got fired? Should I say it again?"

Nothing sanguine is in her voice. One half of his coat's collar falls. "No. That won't be necessary. But, nonetheless, my one dozen—"

"Eyeballs?"

"Yes, eyeballs! My dozen. I was promised it. And...frankly, my students count on me. My students have signed up for eyeball dissection!" In a surge of valor he straightens his posture. She moves her hands to her hips, the large knife remains in her fist, pointing forward, straight outward, toward him.

"You're dissecting eyeballs with students? What kind of a school is this? It's no school my children went to." The second half of his collar falls. The rest of Harry Lime falls with it.

"I...I am Edgar Adam Lugerbauer. Excuse my impropriety. I should have introduced myself first." He holds out his hand. "I am a Professor of Biology at the Academic Gymnasium of Vienna, First District." He stretches his hand farther toward her knife. After a moment she transfers the knife from the right to the left, pulls off her thick leather glove, tucks it into her apron's belt, then grabs his hand for a brief shake.

"Aloisia Klober. Butcher. Right here. Tenth district."

What a hand she has. Muscle. Grip. Strength. Awful. An awful and captivating hand.

"Academic Gymnasium, First District?" she continues as if the words were a foreign language, the First District a foreign land. "Fancy."

"Yes. Proud to say we have nurtured a good part of the country's elite."

"With the help of eyeballs?" Her sharp sneer chops the word eyeball.

"You could say so. The eyeballs play a part. For

example, the eyeball dissection has convinced Dr. Georg
Navratil to pursue medicine. Have you heard of him? An
award-winning opthamalo—"

"I have not heard of him." She looks at E.A.L., her awful arms
folded now, the knife blade sticking from the crook of her elbow.

"In any case, the eyeballs are vital to my educational mission.
And since Jack—"

"He was fired. It's me now."

"Yes, Fr..."

"Frau, not Fräulein, Frau Klober."

"Of course. Frau. You are married. But—"

"I am not married."

"Oh, well. Good? But perhaps you could find it in your heart to
look for these eyeballs. Perhaps Jack had already prepared them.
I spoke to him yesterday." E.A.L. will not give up. He holds up
the carton of his plastic bag with the carton of cigarettes.

"I brought the payment!"

"What kind of payment?" she nods toward the dangling bag.

"Pall Mall. Imported. An entire carton."

"I don't smoke." The bagged carton of cigarettes keeps dangling from his fist. It's worthless. He doesn't smoke either.
What now?

"Are you married?" she asks suddenly, while taking the big
butcher knife by the tip of its blade and tapping the handle
against the side of her leather apron, as if checking the tender-
ness of her own thigh. A solid thigh. A solid and yet tender thigh.

He resolves to give this bewitching awful woman butcher
anything she asks for. Means to an end! Eyeballs first.

"I am... I am... not," he stammers. "I was almost married once, but then we thought better of it. Ha." A pained laugh attaches itself to the end of his sentence. His almost-wife thought better of it, not "we," but who needs to know that? On the eve of their wedding his almost-wife informed him that life with him felt "plotless." Plotless!? No one needs to know that either. He pushes his sliding horn-rimmed glasses back up the bridge of his nose. The Butcheress still dominates his focus and he sees her opening her awful and plump pork-strip lips.

"Do you teach sex stuff too?" She is tilting her head sideways, narrowing her eyes.

"Excuse me?" He swallows.

"Mechanics of sex and such. Biology of the perpetuation of mankind and such. Do you teach that at your Academic Gymnasium?"

He doesn't know what she is getting at. He glances at her lips. They're frightening. Silence.

She slowly—very slowly—slides her knife into the front pocket of her apron. "Well?" Her brows lift, her moss-green eyes spotlight his trembling Adam's apple.

"Yes. Yes, propagation of the species is part of the curriculum," he says, clearing his throat as he promptly remembers the lopsided cross-section of female reproductive organs he drew on the chalkboard during his last painful foray into theoretical sexuality. "Ha. But not in eleventh grade. In eleventh grade we dissect eyeballs. So, if you could,"—he folds his hands to a prayer position—"Help me. Please!??"

Sweat is pearling on his forehead. She finally detaches herself from the doorframe and turns her head. Now he can see her hair poking from beneath the dirty kerchief. An exquisite shade of strawberry blond. Faint wisps of gray. Stunning.

Awful.

"HAS ANYONE SEEN A BAG OF EYEBALLS," she yells into the cavern of the slaughterhouse and, like mooing, from all corners sounds an ominous "NOOO!" She turns around to face him again. Her face now looks like a flesh-made sunflower, beaming.

"Sorry." The Butcheress shrugs her shoulders. "Jack probably took them eyeballs along with everything else." Is she smiling? He blinks at her.

"Do you, do you know where he might have gone then? Jack?" he winces the phrase.

"Where they serve something to drink." She pulls the glove from her apron's belt then slips her naked hand into the stained leather. Has any woman ever worn a glove so hideously attractive? He would like to unglove her. Or disrobe her. And run from her. Slap her face, lick her face, kiss her face. He's never felt such gut-level chaos. He has no use for it. Not now. He stands still. He has to think clearly. Focus on eyeballs. She said Jack could be found where they serve something to drink? That's everywhere! Were he to look into all places that serve alcohol, it would take him days, years. This is Vienna! There are more dives, cafes, and liquor kiosks than fire hydrants. And he knows nothing about Jack, except that he is, he was, a butcher.

Oh now, now E.A.L. can feel his spirit flagging. Jack is gone. And the fog is beginning to lift too. The slaughterhouse brick is turning brighter and the smell of urine is rising from the blood-brown seepage on the cobblestones. Edgar Adam Lugerbauer is not a man who wants to give up, but now he deflates; he sinks into his Burberry. His head falls to his chest, the fedora falls to the grimy floor, leaving his bald spot in full view. For the Butcheress to notice.

Disgrace.

He reaches slowly to pick up his hat. He doesn't look at Frau Klober, the Butcheress, who still stands by the gray heavy door, armed again with her knife. Oh, she can watch him losing his composure in addition to his long-gone plot. He thinks of his students, who are waiting for him, eager to slit a cornea. His one heroic moment a year—gone. Along with his dignity, and Jack.

His stained hat in one hand, the useless carton of Pall Mall in the other, the Professor turns and walks away from her without goodbye, toward the main avenue, toward teaching his class by and with book only.

"Hey! Edgar Adam!" He suddenly hears the exquisitely crude voice of the Butcheress.

He stops. His back to her. Her words whip through his blood with cruel voltage.

Never, never has he heard his name sound so foreboding, so alluring. What now? He expects knives thrown at his back, laughter hurled at his bald head.

"I can get a dozen eyeballs for you by next Thursday. Six-thirty a.m. Bang three times. And bring a Thermos of coffee to share." Then the metal door clangs shut.

He spins around. "What?" She's gone.

Coffee to share? Was this an invitation to more than an

eyeball transfer? He isn't sure. But now he finds himself grinning, a deeply silly and bottomless contortion of his face. Of course he will return with a Thermos! In fact, he will purchase a Thermos and he will make strong coffee, in spite of his excitable sweat glands. He will also wear a better shirt and he will...think of her...of Aloisia Klober, the awful Butcher-Frau.

And the students? The discovery of vision has only been postponed, he will announce, not canceled. It is never canceled!

He begins to walks briskly. Just before he reaches the corner, the sun breaks through the fog and shines on the slaughterhouse.

He sees it.

Roberto Gomez

JEREMY JOHNSTON

Stork

A turmoil in the dirt...a traditional stark gray day. The sky piddles, and an auto wuzzing away, rocking and wobbling, crack, gets exploded in a smoky cough of hell. The mushroom goes up mechanically: like a magic trick, like a vanishing magician. No, Burt thinks, I don't think anyone could survive something like that.

In the gutter of the trench, the teacups brattle and twinkle, shuddering toward the end of the folding card table. One almost topples off into the sucking mud before Timothy, hacking up some mozzarella, catches it and tries to muscle the teetering china back toward the middle with his over-long, damp arms. He looks down at his legs with a curled frown. The buffalo cheese is gulped and Tim watches the percolator rock and gurgle. His nose bulges and his forehead thins to an oval point in various reflections of the silver next to the rinse bin. He returns to his cutlery shuffle. Dinner knifes here: clang. Dessert knifes here: clang. Serving spoons here: clang. Fish knifes here: clang.

This and that.

January twenty-fifth—Welsh Valentine's Day—is appropriately noisy and dreary. A spat has broken out between Paddy—dull, dumb Paddy, sweet crumbs dragged in tracks through his shoulder's sewing, mouth full of damp cake and fists jackaling: This man is going to choke, Burt thinks...ahem, A spat has broken out between Paddy and Anthony, the Italian, who would just have to give the back of Paddy's skull one good whack and his eyeballs would pop out into the shit, Burt thinks, hawking a loogie, nostrils whistling like the seashore. Burt dreads the arrival of the mail, some letter from an obliging Lois whose sincerity will immediately dwindle after the first punctuation mark, he knows. Paddy and Anthony circle each other in what is ostensibly the trench's living room. Paddy grabs the cookie tray from the hob's top, crooks his thumb and forefinger, and throws it tall-ways like a dagger, cookies flying like dominoes, and Anthony catches the hot pan between his khaki knees and stomps it into the mud, which cuts and folds like brownie batter. Anthony bites down onto the back of his American Cigarette with his molars. They're both in helmets.

Out in the mud and the grass, the driver of the auto—who I guess has actually survived—grunts and drags his legless torso dumbly across the ground. The raindrops fall like marbles or tall wet glasses of water. They bend each blade of grass, waxy and striped against the driver's fingertips. The ground wins again: His torso has surrendered one more vital organ by sheer resistance, he calculates, still calculating. He reflects on this too—his calculating, even near death. Any better time? he thinks, out there.

SKRYPTOR

A turd tumbles and swims in the latrine, surely some gravely unfunny joke of Paddy's. The conflict has something to do with said joke and with a lecture that Anthony was giving in direct response. They have both resumed a neoclassical fisticuff posture. Their knuckles are wet.

Anthony spits out his American Cigarette nationalistically and lunges after Paddy with the bottom of his smeary black boot. Paddy's palms clam onto it, and the two buck back and forth maintaining balance à la a human seesaw, Burt thinks: ci-ça, this-that, mhm, he thinks. Anthony pulls out his Webley and fires five shots at Paddy's skull. Fruit forks here: clang. Salad spoons here: clang. Marrow scoops here: clang. Snail forks here: ess-carr-go-go-go. The whole stove-oven arrangement slowly sinks into the stink and the earth. Raindrops clap onto the white hob, fill up the teacups. Raindrop? Drops? Stub and stub: If Tim had toes they'd be soggy, bitter and numb. Trench foot, trench toes. Trench stubs, soggy and sewn. He sits down in the water and looks closely at the ends of his legs. The Colonel will be coming soon.

Burt's cigarette is all ash like a witchy finger, sucks it all in in one drag and puffs out like a smoke box, oily nose observing a slim volume of Tennyson:

> He clasps the crag with crooked hands;
> Close to the sun in lonely lands,
> Ring'd with the azure world, he stands.
> The wrinkled sea beneath him crawls;
> He watches from his mountain walls,
> And like a thunderbolt he falls.
> Burt's maybe bovine, cowish and demure,
> or simply dignified and looking on, eyes colorless.

Anthony flings his revolver at Paddy, who removes Anthony's boot and throws it at Anthony. They briefly catch their breath. Some word describes this small conflict, Burt thinks, specifically the poetry of the small conflict juxtaposed against the significantly larger geopolitical conflict, but he isn't sure of how to arrive at the word so he looks back down at his Tennyson and reads the poem again:

He clasps the crag with crooked hands; close to the sun in lonely lands, ring'd with the azure world, he stands. The wrinkled sea beneath him crawls; he watches from his mountain walls, and like a thunderbolt he falls.

He pulls out a pen and scratches out some of the later words, substituting improvements. Paddy saunters to the mahogany occasional table upon which sits Anthony's goldfish bowl. Burt's nasal exhalations have always seemed to him like a seagull's pale squah, and today the song calls out over the gathering harbor of rainwater in the crotch of his trousers. The barrels of the rifles are wet and smiling.

A faraway machine gun woodpeckers; the bullets twitter and chirp. Anthony unbuckles his helmet and conks Paddy, who has plopped the goldfish into his mouth, on the noggin. Paddy's ass drops into a puddle and the fish flops out between his legs. Anthony puts his helmet back on his head, scoops up the fish and continues his prattling on top of the heap of brown damp rags puddled up in the corner, depositing the fish back into its bowl. The rags smell like mushrooms and rotten eggs. He puts two lozenges in his mouth.

Some very nice china cups clink on a silver tray in Tim's rattling hands, coffee splashing, aubergine boiling in the pot next to the tinned clams. The sound of drunken German folk songs comes from the other side; someone is employing a hurdy-gurdy. Tim walks around shakily, delivering afternoon coffees to the men. Paddy's helmet is sufficiently plopped down over his eyes, still stunned. He fumbles at the edge of it, undoing the strap under his chin and wriggling around in the water. Tim hands him a coffee that he grabs and throws out into No Man's Land; it explodes the moment it clears the ridge. The coffee is somehow, by turn, two different beverages. What is served to Anthony is at least one-eighth incinerated bean, whereas what Burt and Tim are sipping is somewhere shy of weak bathwater. Anthony gulps it down, looks in a glass, combs his hair, and adjusts his mustache. He, again, continues his lecture:

"Which blasted genius conducts this Opera of Nihilism? This dark and dank affair? What, indeed, can the staccato sheep and brassy lion do 'gainst the money-changers, the orchestrators? This grotesque suite now play'd out on gramophone by the pow-der'd, the perfum'd, the rosy, eternally unwhipp'd? These Lords of Sin discuss music, yes, but in trenchant play, nibbling nipples and dashing brains...they have sent out doves and ravens to see who will return from the Symphony of Madness. And who is who? Who's in the fair Ark and who raps on the dark door, mongering? Oh their parlour room—ruby and wretch'd, the idiots—drawn into the able maw of... of... of the Theatre of Blood and Skin and Shrapnel! Seduc'd by the peeking bosom of Bethsheba! To buy her breast you must sell her husband into the smoky shackles of War, yes?

"The Gluttony! The Greed for Death and Death and Death. Lust for the cerebral Ode to Endless War in a crimson sunset!

Each battle a theme, each gun a bow or thread or valve. Each shell the grace note to a falling man. Pluck. It is entertainment and sport and thievery. Let us define the word machinery: Or rather let us define the word clock. Or cuckoo."

The plate of toast and mozzarella runs and spills, and Tim is desperately taking fingerfuls of both into his mouth. He snorts and sort of quacks when he eats, like he's choking. Rain rolls down the glass cover for the cake dish in pearls. The mailman comes by and hands envelopes to Burt and to Paddy who unknowingly slaps his into the mud puddle.

"Colonel is making rounds," the mailman tells Burt.

"'Tsa milk run," chides Burt.

"He has a son now. Yesterday morning—"

"The Colonel?

"Received the cable o'-six-hundred. Wanted you to know: might want some Missus-Daddy." They make extended eye contact. The mailman points at Tim: "What's his problem?"

"Tim?" says Burt, "Thinks he hasn't any feet."

Tim looks at the gray sky and thinks it looks like his father's gray wool trousers when they'd been stained by a splash of mud and street water. His father worked at the Bank of England his entire life, stamping things and coming home sopping wet and cursing, trousers splashed with cloudy gray muddy water, stained and cursing and then eating something and walking upstairs and never coming downstairs again until Christmas morning when he would receive, smiling, a pair of gray wool trousers and everyone would laugh in the living room as snow fell and rose in piles like common bread.

When his helmet finally comes off, Paddy will not recognize the sky as gray at all, but as a stark, stirring white.

Burt's impression of the color gray and of the color of the sky hearkens to a map shown to him in a grade school history classroom where all of the land was sectioned off into puzzle-piece nation-states of variably English-sounding and ethnic-sounding fanciful names, and all of the states were a different color gray.

Anthony thinks the gray sky looks like a big-a, spicy meats-a-ball-a!

Paddy straightens out, clumsily pulls himself together, eyes uncrossing. After some barking and squishing, the Colonel appears, riding crop in hand, thin-lipped. His aide stands beside him. The Colonel is crossed in multiple places by thin leather straps and buttoned down his middle and on his chest with brass emblems, yet he still seems somehow saggy, like he is wearing bagged-up material. His hat is too big and wobbles on his head. The mustache underneath his shiny nose is expertly shaved and looks fake; it is plump in the middle and thins on the outside as though it were a silhouetted pair of pouty lips. He appears to be covered head to toe in goose shit.

"'Nuff willy-waving, you nonce," says Anthony, slapping the back of Paddy's head. "Gentlemen," he says, saluting, vaguely observing his men, "Good morning."

"Good morning, sir!" they cry out, erect and fumbling. Three of the men still have food in their mouths.

"Section report?" the Colonel says, removing his gloves, the length of which—it seems to Burt—make the Colonel's white, bony hands look like ostrich heads with empty eye sockets. The aide's eyes are magnified by his spectacles; his eyes exacerbate his silence.

"Colonel," says Burt, "there was a loud explosion because an auto was blown up out there in the No Man's Land. Maybe ten minutes ago."

"Very good: ours or theirs?" he says, handing his gloves to the aide whose performance has been described as decent and acceptable.

"I believe it was one of ours, sir," says Burt, "and I don't believe there were any survivors."

"Really?"

"The explosion was really quite loud, sir. We all heard it." Tim nods; neither Paddy nor Anthony understands what is happening, hands slippery at their lower backs.

"I see," says the Colonel, tonguing a split lip, eyes betraying an interest in the culinary preparations. "And a, uh, a personnel report?"

"Sir, no significant changes or developments have taken place, sir," then noticing an expectant eyebrow situation from the Colonel, "No casualties, I mean!"

"I seeeee," the Colonel resolved, extending his toes, still looking floppy with, Burt thinks, a somewhat bold attempt at a Heightened Accent.

"Fortunately, through my studies of the literature, sir, I have put together some interpersonal section exercises, sir. Skirmishes are down sixty-five percent."

"Ah, very good. All good news, gentlemen. At ease." The men sort of mock becoming more at ease. "The reason for my visit today is not simply routine. You may have heard that at 0900 hours yesterday my very first son, Domhnall, was born into this world." Tim jumped to applause while Burt ventured a two-handed handshake; Paddy's pinkie was in his ear. Anthony notices the rain lightening, a quiet softening the trench. Through the drizzling breeze he can almost make out the slipping of the driver's khaki against the earth, some twenty meters away.

"Lonnie's father has secured a scholarship for the lad at Cambridge when the time comes," the Colonel gushes, his eyes looking up to the sky in affirmation of the Manifestation of it all.

"Course of study, sir?" asks Anthony.

"Military history is my guess. Alexander. David of Georgia. Napoleon."

"Napoleon," Anthony repeats. "Of course. If you ask me, sir, still a contentious figure."

"My most sincere congratulations to you, Colonel," says Tim, oven mitts on hands. "Would that we had potatoes for the occasion, served in the French custom."

"None of that, none of that," he says, dismissing, sheepish. "But eh—"

"Permission to keep an eye on the baguette, sir?"

"Yes, of course," he says, demeanor melting into gracious humility, "But, ehm, I was thinking that in celebration, we might, ehm...well, I know that as of late there have been, ehm...

what with the nature of, eh, war and the needs of, well, obviously not just men and all that but, ehm...I really don't mean to beat around the proverbial bush here, so to speak," the Colonel said, his posture now having completely wilted, the toe of his right boot needling in the mud. The wind changes slightly, and there is a new stink in each man's nostrils. "Well ultimately, you see, I was just wondering if we might be able to, eh, be... alone...Darling."

Anthony is briefly certain he had seen something prehistoric approaching in the gray sky. The rain has mostly stopped; there are occasional stirs. The mood is meditative. Everything is smelling like the bottom of a dirty lake.

"Of course," says Burt, gesturing quickly to the boys. "Perhaps a bath, Daddy?"

"Oh, darling!" The Colonel exclaims, clapping his hands together. "That is precisely what I'd had in mind."

Anthony and Burt and Paddy start heaving all the eggy rags into a new pile while Tim frantically turns up all the burners, mismatched pots on each one. A lobster pot's been boiling potatoes for hours now; Tim's getting them out with a spatula. An upside-down claw-foot tub is unearthed and flipped over, thunk.

The Colonel unbuckles his belts and straps and rests his hat on the brass coat rack in the corner. He unbuttons his shirt, leaving it on while he undoes his boots. The trousers and undergarments come off, smelly earth running through his toes. Paddy's in the cabinetry toppling from the trench wall, yanking out aprons and bonnets, earrings for himself. Anthony hikes the lobster pot off the burner, hobbles to the tub and empties the steaming potato water into its bed.

"Give it here," Burt mutters to Tim, tying the apron behind him by the sink. He opens the faucet up into the pot, and it fills with milky, silver water. "You get the salts and the ginger from the pantry," he says to Anthony. Paddy has Tim's glass and is caking on a papier poudre, suffering bitten-lip stain in the wet light. Anthony trips over his legs on the way to the pantry; he falls unibrow-first into the mud.

"Georgie?" Anthony gingers.

"Yes, darling," says the colonel, examining a cuticle. "Will you kindly throw me a towel?"

"Bloody hell, Lonnie, did you run out of Hartmann's?" The Colonel deigns to his dropped pants and lobs them behind him in Anthony's direction; they land squarely in black gravy. Tim throws the trousers into the air, where they're punctured by no less than fourteen Madsen rounds. "Darling," mews the Colonel, sitting on the edge of the tub, "do you believe your father thinks me a small man?"

"My sweet, sweet husband," says Burt, upending cold water into the bath, "my father has only spoken of his pride for you, and, on occasion, a not insignificant physical intimidation."

"Intimidation, hmm," he says optimistically.

"He compared you to the Great Philistine!" Anthony lunges toward the tub with the ginger and a cheese grater; Burt tries to mime a Microplane which he feels will be more well received. Paddy, wigged, comes forward with a percolator of hot water and empties it into the bath.

"Only one more, Lonnie," the Colonel requests, "Rather not feel too stretchy. Was the paper delivered?"

"Right-o, darling," handing him a map of Ypres that he reads with great impress. Burt empties one final lobster pot of tapped water into the bath, and the Colonel dips his feet. They redden.

The trench bustles, and the aide stands bone straight, diligently gripping the gloves. Where do babies come from? The seed, it's been said, the seed planted diligently. And the egg must be fertile. The exterior of the egg must be as fertile and penetrable as...as...well, as an embattlement or fortress or stronghold to the Butcher Haig! He rouses within himself! The Guillotine at the Somme. Blood beyond blood: extinction. Yes, he has been to the Crystal Palace and laid eyes upon the terrible dragons. Breathing fire, spiked, scaled, swimming, watching: lizards ten meters long. And of course the men traded cards, drawings... the Great Impotence. Unthinkable beasts powerless against some force unthinkable.

"Lonnie," The Colonel proceeds, the men scrubbing his baby-hair underarms, "I've been giving some thought to... what you mentioned the other night in the intimacy of our darkened chamber."

Paddy eyes Burt, desperately searching for some signal of tactic. Burt's face suggests that this is to be the forlorn hope. Anthony's fingers mingle with the Colonel's toes. Tim pulls burning biscuits—quite literally in flames—out of the oven, black smoke stacking up and out above the trench. The aide dutifully inspects the crack of Paddy's ass.

"There are...histories of...intimacy. In the Orient, men and women are not as conservative around issues of the heart. And body," the Colonel says, winking at Anthony. "I have researched some of what you had professed in ancient Indian literature. Ananga Ranga. Ratirahasya. Kama Sutra."

"I am, eh, aroused, my sweet," winces Paddy, wiping his hands on his evening gown. Paddy is unfamiliar with the majority of the words the Colonel has just used and suspects that Burt's academic penchants have forced this section, these four grown men, into frighteningly cultured territory. Indeed, Burt's expression is one of recalling, not one of outright confusion; Paddy's expression is one of hopelessness.

"At first, I'll admit," says the Colonel, "I was disturbed outright. The prospect of...the nature of your request, the exploration of the sort, any insertion, well, seemed frankly against His will..."

And out in the muddy blades, a tall standing figure looks down at the driver.

"Georgie..." Burt musters.

"Mommy," the Colonel shushes, "tonight, I am ready for it... the Rubber Beak."

The Colonel begins to stand up in the tub, suds running down his jungled groin, his whitewater thighs, while the men with the sponges and towels kneel around him, minus Tim, who's fanning some sweets. The Colonel's legs and back straighten, steaming, rain picking up again. Burt glances down at the claw feet, then at the Colonel's hands, then at the Colonel's head, then at the claw feet again:

"Georgie!"

The bullet sails out of a winking rifle and whizzes across the mossy plot, over the gray grass, over black potholes and a white cloudy eyeball mindlessly taking in the streaky sky: sails across the overturned auto, through and between raindrops and skipping like a small ship, indirigible, eventually and after some time, landing at the tippy-top of the Colonel's nose, right between his eyeballs, mid-blink, and cracking through the bone and skull there before the skin had even broken, smashing the globular bone into at least a million pieces with really just one smack and puncture.

Red blood showers the three kneeling men, Anthony tasting some in his mouth. Paddy can no longer see and grabs Anthony's shoulder, pulling them both backward into the mud. Burt inserts an American cigarette between his lips and lights up. Tim, losing his mind, pacing. Anthony punches Paddy in the teeth, so now Paddy's blood is running out of his mouth and down his front, mixing with the Colonel's blood, but they're of the same red, and now Paddy's boot is in Anthony's groin, and Anthony's hands are clapping down onto Paddy's bonnet. Burt miraculously handles both of their collars trying to pull them apart, American cigarette between his front teeth.

"The Colonel's been shot! The Colonel's been shot!"

"Jesus Christ!"

"Nuff you—"

"Stop this!"

"Jesus..."

"He hit me!"

"Do you see that?" the aide points. "Christ, Anthony—"

"He's—"

"Paddy, shut your mouth, please—"

"That's a petro-daxyl!"

"Get your hands out of there!"

"Git!"

"Slaphead."

"Heavens," Tim exclaims. "What is that?"

The others stop their fiddling and lay eyes on it, out there.

"'Tsa deeno-dino," Paddy says, front-tooth-less.

It walks around the No Man's Land at a meter in height, maybe a meter and a half. It is a feathered dark blue with knobby reedy legs. It bends at the knee to nickel out grubs or critters. From forty meters away, Burt can see it has yellow eyes, yellow with great black holes at their center. It has a beak like an enormous, enormous carrot and splayed feet, ridged and slender and bony like a chicken's. There is silence all down this trench, and there seems to be silence all down that one. The ash tumbles off the end of Burt's American Cigarette like bird shit, his face covered in blood. He spies the driver of the auto out in the in-between, reaching up to pet the bird with both bands, right before it flies away.

IAN CASHEY

For Your Kindness, For Your Buttons

Look at them down there in the alley. Mongrels, three of them, chained to the wall. Rage bulging in their eyes, ready for the attack, a frothy scum hanging from their jowls. What it is they wish to maul limb from limb is beyond what I can see down there in the alley. It seems they've been barking since sunrise and will continue on through the night. Didn't the innkeeper say there's ear cotton at the front counter for an additional fee? I'll have to ask again about that.

She continues showing me the room, the box of matches for the paraffin lamp. She smells of blubber oil, a hefty woman in a bonnet and peasant dress, someone who cracks branches with the same hands she butchers up a caribou stew.

"You'll have to share the bed," she says.

It is a single bed wedged between the wall and a mahogany wardrobe. Made for two people, the top sheet and blanket creased at both ends, a head pillow, inviting you to slide under the sheet with your feet gliding out into the open next to the head of your bedmate.

Ah, how cozy!

To sleep aside the stink of someone else's toe cheese, a dreamer's fungal ambrosia. I can just feel the callous nature of their heels massaging the back of my neck. Say, bedmate, would you mind giving me a wake-up kick to the face? My preference is alongside the jaw.

But wait, wait, there is a touch of civility, a bristle of reassurance, rules to be maintained, when the innkeeper says, "Clean feet, socks required."

She gestures to the sign on the wall.

A simple illustration of a hand sudsing a foot. Beneath the sign is a wooden stool and on the stool is a washbowl with a scrub cloth draped over the edge.

"Spigot's in the alley," the innkeeper says. She is looking at me from the twin mirrors on the doors of the wardrobe. "So you'll be taking the room?"

I don't know.

Will you?

Sarcasm aside, I look to the mirror for consultation, the man looking back at me, a baffled head warped by the mirror, that I would even consider this room.

And the incessant barking of those mongrels, a triple-headed cacophony, a snarling perseverance. Dogs, do they ever go hoarse from all that barking? A guttural resonance, the question continues barking multitudes against the walls of the room.

Yet you smile, a reluctant show of teeth, looking to the innkeeper as you lower the shouldered sling of antlers from your back to settle into the room.

To hear the table-banging fists of rogues and louts gruff with laughter, or someone bashing the head of another with a watered-down mug of ale, this is what I had expected upon entering the Blut Elkken Tavern, surprised to see the oak tables empty, curious to know on a Thursday's eve where these ruffians be?

The bartender shrugs without answer. I choose the table closest to the open fire. Three rows of bench-seat tables. No one here but me and the barkeep and the pot boy who brings me my mug of ale then growls to the brink of biting my hand after I muss his hair to scurry along without a tip.

It is odd, the empty tavern. Could be I'm the early bird and soon the raucous crowd will barrel through the door. So I offer a toast to the flames in the stony hearth. The warmth of the fire makes for fine company, four-foot logs on the iron grate, crackling ablaze a fevered lash.

If only the ale had exceeded my expectations then I'd be brimming with a smile instead of recoiling my tongue from the flat taste of a pond-water scum. Had the bounty of my pocket purse been more, my seat would have been at The Crown, a wingback chair, a frothy blond stout in hand. But the home brew at The Crown is a premium ale at a premium cost.

Blut Elkken's House Rotz Ale?

You can have four mugs of this slosh at the cost of one Crown Ale, or in my case one mug of Rotz for the final scrounge of coins from my pocket purse. What's this on the table? Some such crunch left over from a peppered snack, or the crumbs of a fried scrod—whatever the batter my stomach grumbles for more. Dinner had been a basket of heel bread. Breakfast will be leftovers, one heel in each side pocket of my coat, for the sunrise journey home, twelve hours by foot, or a three-hour coach ride, or the backend of a produce cart, on a lumpy seat of cabbage, should one luck upon a complimentary ride.

But this is how those traveling to and from Grakkas with supplies and produce generate additional income. I could always press the chub of my chest together for a hairy bust. Perhaps then I'd find an eager hand reaching down to offer a ride.

Bleck!

How this swill blisters the tongue. Procured from the drain of your local sewage. Argot Ale. My last trip to Grakkas had been upon a wagon of my own, enough to stock up on a three-year supply of antlers. A quick in, a quick out. Grakkas, where men are known to grow tusks, the only point of civility being The Crown. The rest of Grakkas to the slops, hunters, thieves, mud humpers.

I am a button maker and buck-horn buttons are my specialty. But there is a plague upon us, a scourge of machination, pistons and cranks, powered by a scree of steam, threatening as a corpse grinder to every craftsman, no matter their trade.

The erosion in revenue I incurred last year alone was over sixty percent. See the cavernous wound? Descend if you will. Let's have a look at these shiny little "ditties." I spill the contents from my pocket purse onto the table for inspection—the newest in machine-mouth innovations: the snap-on button.

But, oh, what's this? As quick as they snap together, they snap apart against the strain of anything more than a cuff or a neckline hold. But the tide of market demands continues to flourish at a nauseating pace. We'll take more and make it cheap, cheap, cheap.

Cheap buttons. Cheap ale. Pop goes the waistline. A paralytic crap in the outhouse. But say! Upon purchase. What a shiny button. This brew screws the brain better than any ale.

See, this is the pith of poverty where there is no choice. I know, sitting here, drinking from what I piss. Cheap is all you have. A paper birch hat. Good for torching upon your head should you lose your way in the dark.

I've discussed this with fellow button makers, these inferior buttons, approximating in design the signature of our artistry upon each and every button, at a fraction of the cost, fifty times the speed what our hands can produce. So there's nothing left to do but add to the fire a finger-flicking glitter of snap-on buttons, one flick after the other, until the only thing left for my pocket purse are the buttons of my own making.

Still the question lingers outside the tavern. Where, where these ruffians be? There is no one on the cobblestone road. No horse carriages or pull carts or curbside vendors selling marrow crumbles and sheepskin crackles. The shutters shut to the row of half-timbered buildings. Storefronts and private housing settled for the night. The clock tower too dark to see, though priapic, demonstrative. Oh you mighty tower of time! Shall I grip my groin, give it a waggle in your honor?

There is a rat waddling across the cobblestone road, no dog

chasing after, or filth-laden child with slingshot, or a besotted bard melodiously plucking upon a single-string gourd, congested with song, the rodent's way to Christ. Oh, light me a prayer candle, a Taleggio ooze for Eucharist, that I might spit up the blood of consumption upon your altar.

The Crown is well lit, midway down the road, a broad-chested facade of castle stone, flagpoles angled out front, above the entryway, each one fluttering a griffin of gold upon a background of blue. Is this where the ruffians be? Stripped of their swarthy clothes, scoured and toweled dry, for fine attire and a long-table meal of peppered cordials, sweet meats, and sheepshead pudding.

Opposite where I'm headed, and reluctantly at that, off to nowhere greater than the equine manure plotted about the road. One can only fathom whose feet I'll come to know better than my own as a bedmate. Oh, I beg thee, roll the die in my favor, provide me with a legless roomie, or if he be unctuous as a two-hundred-pound toad, one with socks full of honeysuckle.

Now the true cost of Argot Ale tugs at my bowels, a thorough cough, if one must know, farting crackers. How is it that one's own reek can provide a sense of brute pride? It's emphatic, the noxious heat matching tenor of mind—a vision for you, should the bard pluck upon an encore, a song of heaven's backdoor. Let that be the dream, the gilded entryway to a dimly lit brothel, my burlap sack full of coin, the path cleared to a damask chaise lounge, strumpets coming to my aid from the shadows, buxom in their lingerie.

First, feed me grapes! Then thrust upon my face thy pillows and thy rump that I might gobble my way to divinity.

'Tis a better dream than last—waking with the feast of my fist inside my mouth. Who knew fear of creditors banging on your door could kick into your dreams a glazed head of ham. There's always the dirt you scrape from your fingernails for morning nutrition. And the creditors banging on your door? That was real. How they repossessed the door, the walls, the furniture, if only they had considered me part of the package, then everything would have been fine.

Oh, boo hoo hoo!

They're always hiring at the graveyard, so you shrug, scratch the dander from your hair. From button making to shoveling. Your back can take it. Go on, be a man. Praise that fireball in the sky. You ever hear the sun complaining about age spots or growing too old to shine! Everywhere this night promising as a skin rash, scratch until you bleed. See that tailor-shop window? The one that used to stock your buttons. How about that rock in the road. That doesn't belong out here. That belongs in the tailor shop and then you pick it up, ready for the wind up.

But say, who's this?

Four buildings down, exiting The Crown. He's seen me too, joyous with recognition. "Some other time," you say to the tailor-shop window. How now he calls my name, a young man slowly drifting into focus. Could it be Oleg Krupin? Why, yes! It is Oleg Krupin, son of a wig maker.

The very one who used to frequent my workshop as a boy before moving with his father to Grakkas. Lost his mother to the stopping of the stomach. Final cause of death, fainted in a soap bath after opening her wrists. It was Oleg who cleared the suds, six years old, and I had always suspected suicide because everyone knew she was the wigmaker, Oleg's father an oppressive man, stern and unforgiving, drinking the profits, playing the gifted maker of powdered wigs that after Oleg's mother passed suffered in quality.

I won't lie, many a night I envisioned Oleg's father mysteriously dying so that I might marry Oleg's mother, Isabelle. We would have made a fine pair, but this is speculation, a happy-ever-after wood-block print in the mud, one stomping flat with a sense of guilt, a cold shiver, wondering if there had been something I could have done to intercede? In fact, save Isabelle.

No, no, the story remains, my only interaction with the Krupins had always been from a neighborly distance, except for letting Oleg—after his daily schooling—chisel some afternoons upon buttons of maker's wax.

There was talent even then, his focus upon a side table of work, an intensity that increased after his mother's passing, his father soon drinking himself out of business, moving to Grakkas to become a town fool, forcing Oleg, I had heard, but never witnessed, into working days at a cranberry bog and nights as a tavern pot boy to raise his own father, who eventually drank himself to death, but Oleg.

Look at him now!

A spry young man, snipped of the dead weight of never having had a proper childhood, dancing toward me with a wispy red goatee. See how gently he twirls, arms extended as if wherever the melody leads him there be manna and only manna for him showering from the sky.

He's finely dressed too in factory-spun clothes, a long shirt with a stand-up collar garbed with a broadcloth vest, trousers and knee-high boots, black leather shined to the toe, a reflexive sheen, impressive as the saber belt, upon his hips, a medley of silver pendants.

It's instantaneous, my embarrassment, the sinking lead weight of being outclassed counterbalanced by a radiant sense of pride an uncle would have for his nephew having become such a fine young man.

I glance to where the moths have made meal of my vest and trousers, wishing like a magician for a quick stitch. I don't want him thinking I'm a drunkard, a loose thread on the verge of unraveling, a button maker living in the thistle, cot and tent, near where once his home had been, a home now to a family with an adopted child.

However, it is a half-moon night, impressions to be made more by character and tone than the state of one's wears ringed from the stains of one's pits. I match the width of his arms for a welcomed embrace. Here who once was a boy now deserving of a gentleman's pat on the back.

Do I detect a tincture of orris upon his neck, an opulent musk, or is it upon his breath, the medicinal reek of a top-shelf Scotch. Why, one would need a splinter of gold to pay for such a spirited indulgence. Amazing, how well he seems, standing before me.

How many years has it been since our last seeing each other. It's a question we openly share without answer. I am still stunned by how much he has grown, a head taller than me! Oleg looking down at me, seemingly without surprise, as if he'd been expecting me. My hands still angled high upon his shoulders.

"Well, look at thee," I say, "from pot boy to master."

"Hardly." He winces, edging into a proud smile. "But I would say Jack to Jack."

"Done."

I lower my hands from his shoulders, still gleaming upon his freshly wears.

"Hath ye been courting a maiden this eve?"

"Oh, more striking than that, dinner at The Crown with Sir Edward Finley—as in the Sir Edward Finley of Finley Manufacturing."

"Oh?"

Then Oleg stiffens before me with a triumphant turn of the chin and shoulder. "You, good sir, are standing before the new lead mechanic of Finley Manufacturing."

"Well, now. That's so?"

"Why, indeed." Oleg continues spreading the news before me with an open show of hands. "From buckles to buttons to zippers. That's our trade."

"Buttons!"

"I know, not good for a maker such as thee." And he does appear troubled, treading upon a hunch, leaning in closer. "But certainty would have me guessing you're retired. No?"

"Certainty?" My smile hardens.

Oleg, such a young man, the entirety of his life ahead of him, freed from the gravity of his father's strife. Why present him with a struggle of my own? Nothing there he need know of my final ambition as gravedigger so I nod.

"Of course, of course. Why, this past year, upon a small bounty I roost. These cramped fingers freed of all button making."

I open my hands, stretching my fingers wide. This incites laughter and again I can smell the medicinal reek of Scotch on his breath. Enough to want a gulp myself. I can even hear the screech of silverware from the dinner he must have cut into with Sir Edward Finley. Then I add to my bogus retirement more proud-chested lies: a chalet, travel plans, time to practice a craft from the Orient.

"Perhaps, you've heard of it?" I say. "Or-i-gami, much gentler on the hands."

I tell him of a wolf I made from a sheet of paper while my hands tell a different story, thinking of those machines he's been hired to maintain, those machines spitting at me, buttons, buckles and zippers!

My desire for the eradication of manufacturing trembling in my hands hidden by the false excitement of this origami ruse: "Once you crease the jawline and ears then you'll have a wolf, and if you tug the tail, oh, how he howls!"

"Such miracles I'd like to see," Oleg says. "Someday you should show me."

"Of course, of course."

"So you're here for the drunken mile?"

"Excuse me?" I look behind me as if he's speaking to someone else.

"The drunken mile," Oleg says. "Twelve Argot Ales to step up to the starting line. Tomorrow this cobbled road after the race will be nothing but vomit and blood."

"Ay, so that's where the ruffians be this eve? Saving themselves for the drunken mile. What's the prize?"

"Hmmm, a month's worth of port and bread, a Stilton wheel

of cheese."

"I'm already turning blue."

"So you won't be running?"

"Bleck, no!"

We share the laugh of two men confounded by such an aloof sport, for the clowns, and cockeyed drunks. But it could be a good send-off, twelve Argot Ales taking me to the finish line of Grakkas, head-spanked with a grin finding a bush to sleep behind before making it a mile upon the forested road.

Then Oleg tells me of his wife, a successful seamstress, expecting too, and it is touching to hear, producing in me a lengthy sniffle, enough to become misty eyed, thinking of one supporting the other. What more could one hope from a marriage? Oleg more of a man than his father had ever been, even more than myself.

To be married, a possibility I had skipped over more than once, never once bending on my knee to propose, but bending on my knees, yes, to scramble beneath the bed of a married man before he barged in upon his wife. I must admit the excitement did flow harder beneath that bed than it did upon it. Perhaps that's what I had loved more than love itself. The risk of being caught! But slick as the oils I had glossed over many a slender leg—never was I caught, until I caught a lapful of open sores, the winnings of a lusty ambition, but to Oleg it's clear I'm a civil man, and with him here helps me to stand as such, even beginning to believe it myself, after he thanks me for my kindness, for my buttons, for the afternoons I had let him work upon the side table in my shop.

Then there is a beggar, wheezing before us, who ceases to

rattle his can, holding it before Oleg.

"Can you spare me some coin?" he says his mouth black with rot.

Oleg obliges without question.

Two coins, plink, plink inside the can.

Then the beggar turns to me.

"You, sir?"

Oleg seems expectant too, and I don't want him thinking me miserly, so I am quick to produce my pocket purse, obscuring the glint of my donation, three plinks inside the can, pronouncing me a generous man, more so than Oleg. The beggar's eyes widen with thanks.

"Blessed be you both good men."

Then off into the night, he oddly hobbles, while between us the soiled reek of many a homeless night continues to pervade to the degree where we side step several steps to finish our conversation upon fresher air.

"So tomorrow alpine climbs for you," Oleg says. "A rocking chair, I imagine, evergreens to ponder. The life of a retiree."

"Not entirely." I waggle my finger. "Origamis to produce."

"Yes, yes," Oleg says with a simper of laughter, pocketing his hands. There is a sadness upon his eyes he cannot hide and it's in this silence between us I wonder if he sees in me the ghost of his drunken, buffoon of a father, a man who had been known for trumpeting on a flugelhorn lies, a grandiose vision of the life he lived when anyone seeing him would know he was but a fool. Then Oleg asks if I'd like to meet his wife, even stay the night. He seems insistent, though I tell him with yawning arms my room at The Crown is waiting for me and from that there is the assurance of our meeting another time.

"And then for the little one," I add, "a wolf from paper I shall make, or perhaps a swan."

And our final hug is one of warmth, congratulatory toward the other. It's not all bad where I'm going, a room with whose feet I'll be sleeping next to I don't know. But it's not upon these roads with manure for a head pillow. Then we walk our separate ways and I think of a lost life I could have had, had I the courage, the fortitude, the faith. I had always had eyes for Isabelle, but never more than that, only eyes. Could it have been more? I'll never know.

Now I am approaching The Crown and can still see Oleg behind me upon his journey home. I wish he would turn from the main road, so that he doesn't see me feigning entry into The Crown. I could stand in the lobby, say I'm waiting for someone, when I see from across the road, the beggar scuttling toward me from out of a darkened alleyway.

"You, you, you give me these buttons!"

I back against the door of The Crown.

"You, you, you make a mockery of me?!"

He has me by the shirt, the anguish in his eyes deep upon mine. It's a scene, I am thankful upon glancing sidewise, Oleg will not have to see, this deranged man of half my strength throttling me against the door of The Crown, reinforcing the fact he doesn't need my stinking buttons and to that I will think days later, after the door to The Crown opens to a guardsman prodding us like wild beasts with a lance, "You are not alone." But in this moment this beggar has me against the door all I can do is surrender to the throttling rage of his hold, my back knocking repeatedly against the door, as one would, demanding to be let in.

IAN CASHEY

Jenna Cha

DAVID M^cCLELLAND

Brothers

Our parents left the house to both of us, but Alex didn't want
any part of it. The nights before and after the funeral he stayed
at a new motel just off the highway. The building was completed
but the signs and the decorative cornices were yet to be added
and there were still cranes and front-loaders on the scraped
earth that would be the parking lot.

When I came to pick him up for the service he wouldn't let
me into his room because he had someone with him. I sat on
the couch in a lobby that smelled sourly of the breakfast buffet's
weak coffee and watched the elevators. He was alone when the
doors opened and he came out wearing a dark blue suit and
baby blue shirt and a silk tie patterned with the yellow, white
and purple of violets.

"Is it someone you brought with you?" I asked. "Am I going
to meet him?"

"Of course not," Alex said. "No one would come with me all
the way out here. For a funeral. If I hadn't needed a drink last

night he'd be waking up alone. And I'm not letting him get a look at the two of us together either."

"Why not?" I asked.

"Because a guy like that," he said. "If he knew I had a twin, he'd get all kinds of ideas."

Some time after the funeral an envelope came to the house. Inside were keys and a letter, which read, My dearest, only brother. A man has asked me if I want to travel with him and I thought about it and I do want to. He's older than me, he's made his money, and now he wants to spend it. Or some of it. It would be hard to spend it all, even for me. I know what this will make you and probably everyone else say about me. And that opinion of me might even be the correct one. But so what? I'm still going to do it.

We both know I owe you for everything you did for our parents. So now I'm in a position to give you something. What I can give you, if you want it, is the life I've been living here. You'll have to see if it means anything to you, if it's worth more than the life you already have. I can give you my job, which is an okay job, considering, and my apartment. If that sounds good to you, then just come on. But it would be easiest if you did it quickly.

Take anything of mine that might be useful to you. Anything at all. Everything is now yours as it was mine. How's that? You can take my name and trash it. Or redeem it, more likely. You can be the Doctor Jekyll to my Edward Hyde.

If you come here you might meet another man whose name is also Alex. Well, probably you will meet him. You can tell him

I'm sorry, because I am. But that's another thing that doesn't matter because I'm going no matter what. At least he won't be disappointed. Or he might be disappointed but he won't be surprised. I think there's probably a specific word that accurately describes what Alex is going to feel, because it's a singular feeling, but I don't know what the word is. It's the feeling that comes when something that you know is false, but that you want to be true, is finally revealed to be the lie you had wanted it not to be. Make sense? I've had that feeling about myself. Maybe you have too, or had it about yourself. It's not uncommon.

Still your brother, Alex

I was never able to get away while our parents were sick, and I hadn't been to the city in all the time Alex had lived there. One of the first things I saw when I left Grand Central was a pretty girl in a short skirt and knee-high plastic rain boots, smiling at me. But when I turned to smile back at her she had gone and there was a soot-faced man sitting in a collapsed trash can, holding a torn piece of nylon in his hands.

Alex's apartment door had just a single lock, set into the doorknob, as insecure as the lock of a closet door or a toolshed. I reached in and found the light switch, and stood in the doorway looking at a shrunken kitchen and a bathroom with a pink shower curtain for a door. A window showed the window of a like apartment set into a brick wall not two feet away.

The apartment had the meaty stink of cat shit, and just beyond the curve scraped into the dark green floor tiles by the edge of the opening door were a few tan oblongs and a greasy liquid that had found its own shape in the cracks and divots of the linoleum. A small gray cat came out from somewhere and sat down with all four paws together and looked at me.

"Here, kitty," I said.

I held out my hand but the cat startled up and cantered away through an open doorway. The apartment's second room was barely bigger than the bed that filled it and the cat was gone from sight.

The bathroom was too small for a sink. The toilet faced the shower stall and in the bit of floor space between them was a pan of cat litter and a bowl that had recently held water and a white bowl smeared with dried cat food. Taped to the wall was a piece of paper with a pencil drawing of a cat, and written below the drawing was the name Timothy.

I didn't like that name for a cat, so I changed its name to Tiny. I said, "Here, Tiny."

The cat didn't come out. In the refrigerator was an open can of cat food with a fork in it, and nothing else. I filled the white bowl with the wet food and rang the fork off the bowl's edge and the cat came out. I said, "Here, cat. Your new name is Tiny. Have some food."

I ran a finger down the cat's spine while it ate and it flinched but it let me.

"I guess he was sure I would take his offer," I said. "He bet your life on it."

Alex had given me two addresses in his letter. In the morning I went to the second. A doorman in uniform and hat saw me coming and opened one of the building's brass-trimmed double doors for me and smiled.

"Good morning," he said. "Bright and early today."

I looked back at him as I waited for the elevator and he was still smiling at me, and I didn't know why. Was it him? Or was it me? Or was it Alex?

At the fourteenth floor the elevator opened onto a small foyer whose walls were enameled from baseboard to molding in mother-of-pearl cut into even, finger-length rectangles. There were two unnumbered doors and I knocked at both but there was no answer. I pressed the buzzer and heard a bell ringing far away. Finally, I tried the door handles and one door opened, letting me into a cool and plum-colored apartment whose windowed walls held views of the city and of the park and the rivers surrounding the island, and on to the horizon.

I went through the apartment's many rooms. No one was there. Off a dark study where an enormous television faced a curve of low couches was a thin rectangle of a room that might once have held linens, with a single window opposite the door, two walls of dark bookshelves filled with labeled binders, and a shallow built-in desk. A flat silver frame on the desktop held a picture of Alex, very young, standing between our father and mother in the yard of the house we had grown up in. A matching picture still stood on the mantel of the house, showing our father and mother and myself at the same young age standing between them. Once there was a picture that included all four of us, but that had been put away.

Stacked on the desk were three screenplay manuscripts. A note written in Alex's hand said, "For Alex to Read."

I was sitting in the desk chair and making my way through the topmost manuscript when I heard people coming into the apartment. I sat looking at the doorway of the small room. Would Alex get up to greet them, or would he wait for them to come to him? Did it matter? No. What I did now would be what he would do. Whatever I might choose.

A man walked past the doorway carrying a suitcase and a garment bag and a pink-and-white-striped hat box, tied with a pink and white ribbon.

"Hey Alex," he said.

I raised my hand but he was gone before I could have said his name, even if I had known it. After a few minutes he came back and leaned in the doorway.

"Hey buddy," he said.

"Hey," I said.

"She's on her way up. Look busy."

He gave me a grin to let me know he was joking. He was in his fifties at least, with a brush cut, wearing gray pants and a white shirt and a blue jacket. His jacket was open and there was a small gun in a brown holster on his belt.

"How was your trip?" he asked.

"Oh," I said. "You know. Pretty okay. How was your weekend?"

"I don't remember," he said. "So I guess it must have been something. Right?"

"Right," I said.

"Gotta get back to the car," he said. "Double-parked. Be good."

"Okay."

After a while there was the sound of another person in the apartment. I listened as they came through the different rooms. Finally a woman appeared in the doorway and stood there with her arms outstretched.

"Alex," she said. "You've returned."

She was wearing what I thought at first was an evening gown, but which was in fact a kind of generously cut pantsuit. A dark silk scarf hung from her shoulders like a cape. Her clothes were made of soft fabrics in dessert colors, chocolate and plum and cream. Her black hair was shining and long and brushed back from her face. Impossible to tell her age. She stood there with her arms out, waiting, and I realized her pose was not just theater. I went to her and we embraced and kissed each other on both cheeks. She held me by my shoulders at arm's length and looked at me. She passed her palm along my temple.

"How are you? You look good. You look different somehow. Fresh. Did you get your hair cut? You must have gotten your beauty rest," she said. "So how was your trip. Relaxing?"

"I think so. Yes."

"I want to hear all the stories."

She saw the manuscript on the desk.

"How are the scripts. Anything good? Any diamonds in the rough? Any pearls before the swine?"

"Not yet."

"Well. I'm leaving you be. I'm in my office. If you find any Oscars just ring the bell."

"All right," I said.

Near lunchtime I came to the end of the first script and to make a record of having read it I wrote a summary on a piece of paper and clipped it to the title page. I was reading the second script standing up to stretch my leg muscles when the doorbell rang. From somewhere in the apartment the woman said, "I'll get it." I heard her going at nearly a run to the front door. There was the sound of her voice and a man's voice excitedly talking over each other, and then she called out to me.

"Alex," she said. "It's your Alex."

I stood and waited and he appeared in the doorway. He was taller than me, but not as old as I thought he might be. He wore a blue suit with a fine light blue stripe, a white shirt with an embossed pattern, and leather lace-up shoes the color of butterscotch that matched his belt. He stood in the doorway with one hand on the frame and looked at me but not directly. As if only seeing my shape against the window behind me.

"Well," he said. "I hope you had a very nice trip."

This was the third time I had been asked that question this morning, but he wanted an answer.

"Alex," I said.

"What," he said quietly. "You know, on the way here I was even worried for you. That I would get here and you wouldn't be here and you wouldn't have called in and she wouldn't know where you were because something had happened to you. I thought we were past all this shit. I can't be chasing after you all the time. I can't even be here now. Plus not sleeping. One way or another it's got to stop."

"Alex," I said again. "Wait a minute. Listen to me."

Something in my voice got to him. He became very still and stood with his chin up as if listening to something he could barely hear. He reached inside the office next to the doorframe and hit a switch I had not known was there and a spine of lights lit in the ceiling and brightened the entire room. He stepped up to me and looked me up and down. He fingered the cuff of the shirt I was wearing as if he were checking the material on clothes worn by a mannequin, took my right hand and looked at the back of it and flipped it and looked at my palm. He reached as if he were about to touch my hair, as if he wanted to push it off of my forehead or to the side, but instead he stepped back and leaned in the doorway.

"Listen," I said.

The life came back to his face and he stood up straight.

"She doesn't know who you are," he said.

"No," I said.

"Then let's go. Let's go to lunch. She expects us to. You can do that. You can go to lunch with me."

"Of course," I said.

We went out to the small foyer and he pressed the button for the elevator before calling into the apartment.

"Bye Martha," he said. "We're lunching."

"Lunching," she called back. "Bye, sweetheart. See you soon, Alex."

Alex looked at me.

"See you soon," I said.

We did not speak on the ride down. The doorman opened the door for us and smiled but I did not meet his eye. On the street Alex started walking and I followed. We passed a restaurant with a bright blue awning.

"That's a place we like to go," he said.

We turned a corner past a café with tables out on the sidewalk and a young hostess standing at a wooden podium with menus in her hand.

"They have very nice salads," he said.

He stopped at a deli. Plastic signs filled the windows.

"This will do," he said.

As we went in he pointed at two empty stools at the counter that ran along the window and told me to take those.

I sat and waited. He came back and put a brown paper bag in front of me and sat down.

"I'm sorry," he said. "This is where I would have brought him. As a punishment. But you and I could have eaten anywhere."

"It doesn't matter."

"You look goddamn just like him."

"I know. How did you know it was me and not him?"

"Suddenly I just knew. And then your clothes."

"But they're his clothes. From his closet."

"I know it. But he wouldn't wear those pants and that shirt together. In fact he doesn't wear that shirt at all any more."

I looked at my lap. The shirt was blue and the pants were brown.

"In fact I gave him that shirt," he said.

"I'm sorry."

"It doesn't matter. Of all the things, that doesn't matter at all. Listen. I need to know. Is this just for fun? Is this just a lark? Is he coming back?"

"I don't know."

"Of course you know."

"He's not planning to. No."

Alex took two sandwiches and two bottles of seltzer out of

the paper bag and set one of each in front of me.

"You know," he said, "if this were happening to someone else I would think it was quite fun. I mean it could be quite fun. I could give you wardrobe tips and tell you the names of old friends and little stories about them so you don't look stupid when we meet them on the street accidentally. We could go to parties and you could pretend to be just however I wanted you to be and you'd never know the difference and neither would they. It could be fun. A comedy. A bedroom comedy."

He put his hand on my knee and leaned toward me.

"You would be distraught from the recent deaths in your family. I would be the only person you knew in the whole great big city. I would be your knight in shining armor. Coming to your emotional rescue."

"Like the song," I said.

"Like the song."

After a moment he took his hand from my knee.

"I'm sorry," he said. "Forgive me. I'm not behaving well. You didn't come here just to hurt me."

"I didn't come here to hurt you at all," I said. "I didn't even know about you until he wrote me last week."

"Oh," he said.

He sat and looked at the clutter of plastic signage covering the window. He opened his seltzer and put a straw in it and the bubbles lifted the straw out of the bottle and tilted it into the air. The elbows of people lining up to buy lunch were pressed into our backs.

"Well," he said. "There it is. I thought it was bad already. But. I didn't even matter enough for him to tell his twin brother

about me. That must be the saddest thing that's going to happen.
It must be. Nowhere to go but up now."

"He told me to tell you he was sorry. He said if I saw you to
tell you he's sorry."

He lifted his eyebrows and shrugged.

"If you knew where he is, would you tell me? Or did he ask
you not to."

"I don't know."

"Do you know who he's with?"

"Someone older," I said. "Older and with money. He said you
wouldn't be surprised."

"No. It was either that or read about it in the obits. I'm sorry.
Forget I said that. You should eat your sandwich. It's a good
sandwich here, believe it or not."

"Okay."

"So," he said. "What about you. Is this a permanent move?"

"I don't know. Maybe."

The whole time he had been looking into my face, watching
me as I talked and moved. Now he looked away.

"I have to go," he said, and stood up.

I stood also. Half a sandwich in my hand.

He said, "No. Stay. Finish your lunch. Finish my lunch if you
want. Listen. I'm sorry about your folks. Really. From me to you.
I'm sorry. They seemed like pretty good people. Little trouble
with, you know. With modern life, I think."

"Yes," I said.

He looked at me again, and then away, and told me goodbye
and went out. A woman in a navy blue skirt and a silk shirt
with a black ribbon tie took his place. I finished my sandwich

and put his sandwich and the seltzer waters back in the paper bag and left the deli. I gave the bag to a man with sunburned knuckles and a sunburned bald spot wearing a green ski jacket and sitting against a fire hydrant.

"Thank you," he said.

When I left Martha's for the day a gray matting of rain clouds had overtopped the buildings. I passed a stooping, white-haired man standing bareheaded in the rain. He was holding a disconnected payphone receiver at arms length and whispering at it. The silver phone cord dropped straight down and colored wires frayed from the end. The man stood knee-deep in a raft of overstuffed yellow plastic bags, blooming up from the wet black pavement like flowers from a marsh.

In the apartment Tiny was sitting neatly centered in the doorway to the bedroom and again the place smelled like raw cat shit but there was nothing on the floor. I looked in the pan by the toilet and there was a beige pyramid centered on the green and white cat litter. Still wet and stinking. I dropped layer after layer of toilet paper over it until it stopped seeping through and then I picked it up and tried to flush it and the toilet clogged.

I woke in Alex's bed. The alarm clock read 2:36. Coming out of sleep I was sure it was him I had heard opening the apartment door, so I went to the kitchen wearing only the underwear I had slept in and there was a girl standing there rocking Tiny in her arms like a baby. The cat's eyes went large and startled at the sight of me. The girl wore maroon sweatpants and a sleeveless

white T-shirt with pink frill at the armholes and was barefoot
and not wearing a bra. When she saw me she dropped the cat
and came at me and hugged me hard, and I could smell her hair
and her perfume and a sweet smell of alcohol.

"Alex," she said.

I didn't put my arms around her, and she stepped back. She
was still wearing the evening's makeup.

"I'm sorry. I woke you up. Welcome back. I just came up to
feed Timothy."

"Tiny," I said. "I changed his name."

She looked at the cat standing at her feet with its back arched
to be petted.

"Well," she said. "How was your trip? How's Alex?"

I sat on one of the two kitchen chairs.

"Listen," I said. "I don't know you."

She stood still and looked at me.

"I'm not Alex. Alex is my brother. He's gone away with
someone."

I could see the import of what I was saying getting through to
her in discrete realizations. She was drunk in her nightclothes
in an apartment with a nearly naked stranger.

"Jesus. Does Alex know?"

"Now he does."

She crossed her arms. "Jesus."

"Who are you?"

"I," she said. "You don't know. Of course not. Susan. I live
downstairs. I watch Timothy when you go away. When Alex
goes away. Tiny."

"Does he go away a lot?"

"Sometimes. Sometimes I spend the night here. To get away from my roommate and her boyfriends."

She stood with her bare feet together on the linoleum.

"So I guess you're going to feed the cat from now on?" she said.

"Yes."

"Okay. Good night then."

"Good night," I said.

I stood up to open the door for her but she opened it herself and went out. I heard her go down the hall and down the stairs and then a door opened and shut. I went to the bedroom and put on a T-shirt and Alex's black sweatpants and came back to the kitchen and sat and Tiny jumped up to sit at the end of the kitchen table and look at me.

I heard her come back up the stairs and she knocked on the door to the apartment and I let her in.

"You can ask me whatever you want," I said. "But I probably won't know the answers."

"Is Alex with Tony?"

"He's with someone older with a lot of money. Is that Tony?"

She sat in a kitchen chair and Tiny stepped from the table to her lap. "Is he coming back?"

"He's not planning on coming back."

"How are you going to pay for this. You're not on the lease. The building won't take your checks."

"He left me his checks. And his credit cards. And his driver's license."

"He left his driver's license?"

"Yes."

She sat and petted the cat.

"You're not the same," she said. "I can see it now that I know."

She took the cat from her lap and put him on the table and left the apartment. I waited but she did not come back and I shut off the overhead light and went back to bed.

When I woke again she was standing at the end of the bed in the narrow bedroom. No lights on in the apartment. Like something I was dreaming. I stayed still but she saw that I was awake and came into the bed. I moved to give her room and we lay looking upward.

"Sometimes I spend the night here," she said. "With Alex. After parties. Or if one of us can't sleep we'll stay up together. If he doesn't want me to come in he ties a little ribbon on the door handle."

I lay there and listened to her.

"You used to do this all the time," she said. "He told me about it. You'd switch classes and no one would know. You could switch girlfriends and no one would know."

"If they knew," I said. "They didn't mind."

Lying there looking up into the dark box of the ceiling my voice seemed not to be my own, and the words not ones I was speaking but only ones I was hearing.

"Everyone expected you to switch at your graduation so you didn't and they all thought you did anyway."

"Yes."

"And then the same college. Until your parents got sick. You switched classes as you pleased. Not just for hijinks but to test out each professor and share your notes and get the best grades you could."

"Yes."

"So I shouldn't be surprised. I should have seen it coming."

Her shoulder was touching mine, and her hip and her feet. She rolled onto her side and put a hand on my stomach and looked at me laying looking upward into the dark.

"You know I've seen you naked," she said.

"Alex."

"Yes. Lots. He likes being seen. Coming out of the shower and getting dressed in front of me. Which is fun for me. And I've tried to give him a hug or a little squeeze sometimes but he just doesn't like that from me. But you like it."

"Yes," I said.

She had her hand beneath the waistband of my shorts and I helped her by sliding them all the way off. She paid careful attention to my body as if satisfying a great curiosity, and rather than letting me touch her freely she showed me just how she wanted me. Later in the night she wanted to hold hands and we did and she began crying.

I woke again when the door shut and I was alone in the bed. I didn't know what apartment was hers, so in the morning I wrote notes with her name and Alex's phone number on them and slid one under the door of each apartment on the floor below, but she never called.

Alex occasionally writes, and sometimes sends things. He sent me a Piaget Altiplano, but I've left it in its box, and once he sent an envelope with fifteen hundred dollars in fifties. Marsha has not stopped calling me Alex. Steven, her bodyguard, is a

LUMINOUS VOLUMES

retired homicide detective with a lot of stories. Funny how many people go to jail for killing their parents. Also funny how often a screenplay will tell a story similar to mine. I haven't gone back to the house, but if I'm Alex I never have to. His name isn't on any of the paperwork.

One night I was going out through the subway turnstiles in a push of people. The crowd on the other side was waiting with tokens in their hands to go through and try for the train, which was already closing its doors. Someone went by me and said something into my ear and I felt a quick slap-slap-slapping at my back. I stopped where I was and turned to see what was happening behind me, and on the platform just the other side of the turnstile a man much shorter than myself was holding a clean, neatly addressed oversize envelope in both hands and staring straight into my face. His ears pulled back and mouth partly open to show his teeth. Looking fixedly at my face but not into my eyes. He was calling me motherfucker. "Yes you, motherfucker. Fuck you, motherfucker." Then he went on. Insulting every one of the differences which were immediately remarkable between us and making up other subjects to curse as he stood there.

"Listen," I said.

He abruptly shut his mouth and then just as abruptly started up again about how this motherfucker wanted me to listen, motherfucking bitch. All this happened in less than a moment. I stepped forward to stand in the turnstile with just the locked bar between us. I heard a kid say, "Ooh, there's gonna be a fight." The man was cursing just out of arms reach but looking tense enough to jump at me.

I stopped trying to talk over him and let myself just look at him. He wore at least three T-shirts, layered under a plastic windbreaker whose rips were fixed with white gaffer's tape. He would not make eye contact with me, so I was free to look closely at his face. The grizzle along his jaw where he had missed while shaving. The lines on his forehead and the one line that was too strong and must be a scar. The deep pockets under his eyes and the whites of his eyes gone yellow. He was older than I had first thought, with gray curls in his hair and loose skin under his chin. All the individuated markers of his own face. His eyes were wide with the rage he was slipping into, his lips were dry, and sweat was starting to show on his forehead. His own face.

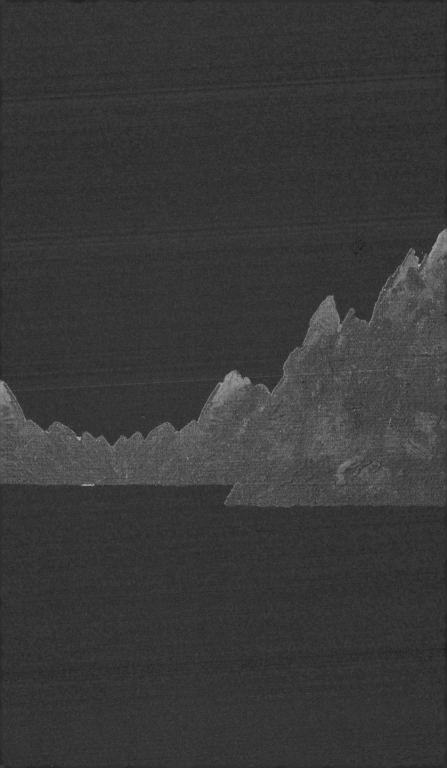

SURFIN' TURF

THE HOPELESS ARTIST 2014

SARAH BLANK

Surfin' Turf

It was June gloom in late July when the predawn crew paddled out. You'd see them stretching and yawning, lugging their long-boards from woodies and assorted shit boxes into the mirrored Pacific sunrise.

After sunup, there'd be scads of surf guys in the water—a friendly stew of old timers who'd caught surf fever when they'd been stationed in Hawaii and teenage dudes with summers to burn. They would stick around until the sun seared off the haze, snoozing on the sand or chasing beach-bunny tail. But that was later. Morning was hallowed time for surf riding and nothing but.

But these days, it wasn't uncommon for someone's primal shrieking to punctuate the rhythm of the breaking surf. Today it was Da Mute, wailing raggedly out on the jetty, tightly rocking with his head in his knees.

Ditching his board, Butchie swam as fast as he could against the tide. Pulling himself onto the jetty, Butchie caught a wave of revulsion. It hit him hard—why Da Mute was screaming his head off. Why Corky had been a no-show that dawn. Butchie surveyed what was left of Corky. Sun-bleached, wise-ass Corky. Corky, who'd teach you how to walk the nose and shoot the curl. Corky who'd give you a ride anywhere in his '48 Jeep if it wasn't already packed to the gills with his cute cousin and her surf-honey friends, all of whom he was balling.

Butchie doubled over and retched. They'd finally gotten Corky. His balsa board was snapped in two. Splayed on one half were Corky's baggies—duck canvas numbers stained brown with blood. Piled on the other was a slimy mound of kelp and guts—the parts of Corky that were too unappetizing and labor intensive for their yield. Topping it all off were Corky's gray eyeballs, giving goofy life to the sad heap.

And there, below the broken surfboard, Corky's waterlogged fingers and toes formed two stubby words:

LOCALS ONLY

You've probably heard tell that as a species, mermaids can be supreme assholes. And for the most part, you're not wrong.

Mermaids are pod-centric pleasure-seekers with a flair for the lurid. They have finicky taste in what they kill and eat. They'll smother a full-grown halibut just to pick at its cheeks.

They'll dive down into the deepest depths on late night raids, muscle a 100-pound moonfish, bore a hole in its side and take turns drinking warm blood, siren lips pressed to lunar belly.

Mermaids' salmon-pink hair comes from carotenoids in shrimp, their snacky mainstay. Ghost shrimp, mantis shrimp, pink shrimp and brown shrimp—all of whose sweet insides the mermaids extract, scramble and restuff into their respective carapaces before downing whole.

This is all to say that the unincorporated stretch between Los Angeles and Orange Counties was prime feeding grounds for the Pacific mermaids. For millennia, pods of mermaid huntresses dove in tandem through El Porto's rich underwater canyon, spearing and stacking prey to bring back to their dens.

Southern California's waters were excellent spawning grounds too. In those days, there was no shortage of South Bay Toothfish males eager to do their procreational part. You see, despite what you've heard, there's no such thing as Mermen. No, when the special time comes in a young mermaid's life to spawn, she seeks out a South Bay Toothfish male to do some tender mouthbrooding.

First, the Toothfish males dig sandy nests for huntress mermaids to deposit their eggs.

The male Toothfish externally fertilize or "bust milt all over" those eggs, then collect them in their mouths, paternally incubating the eggs and forgoing all food until the mermaid pups hatch.

Using their razor baby teeth, the pups then gnaw their way through their mouthbrooder Toothfish hosts. The pups' frantic mewling signals their grandmothers to collect the precious younglings from the Toothfish carcasses.

Thankless as this endeavor sounds, this is just one side of the Mermaid-Toothfish quid pro quo. The male Toothfish volunteered themselves in exchange for the mermaids' guaranteed protection of the female South Bay Toothfish and their offspring. The mermaid colony encouraged the pregnant, freshly jilted Toothfish widows to make its den their haven, to stow their larvae on the rocky floors until the juvenile Toothfish were ready for deeper waters. Through this symbiotic do-si-do, both mermaids and South Bay Toothfish assured their continued propagation.

And there's no great mystery to the physical act of mermaid reproduction or for that matter, mermaid excretion. Simply stated, mermaids have an all-purpose vent below their caudal fin. For all the high drama and gustatory specificity lavished on what mermaids ingest, no shame and very little attention in general is paid to business on the other end. The rule of fin is conventionally, don't shit where you eat but the qualifier is: The sea is vast, the sea washes away all sins.

This logic was not unique to mermaids. As soon as Los Angeles was populous enough to call itself a city, its fair citizenry opted to construct a network of pipes and tunnels with a terminus in El Segundo, its outflow shooting raw turds into the gaping mouth of the Pacific. In 1950, they opened a treatment plant on the same grounds, making the resulting sludge a little less raw. This slightly less-putrid effluent and the resulting rise in water quality flooded the shore with novice surfers, all eager to have at the waves that swelled from the undersea canyon, persistent pink eye and bouts of the squirts be damned.

At first, the mermaids largely ignored the surfers. There were so few of them and those few were so inept, the best thing to do was to find a primo vantage point and behold the sloppy rodeo of men riding homemade boards over the bucking humps and slumps of the waves.

Corky was one of those pioneering masochists. He crossed

his heart and swore to Butchie he'd seen a pair of fat topless grannies gawking at him in the swells. The bathing beauties cackled at his expense then vanished, diving into the barrel of a wave.

Mostly though, the mermaids kept out of sight. Those who left the den spent their days farther out in the open ocean, periodically trawling the deeper waters along the strand.

Nighttime was for one-eyed snoozing in clusters, sheltered by the bone-lattice walls of the den. Nestled between derelict pier chunks, barnacled industrial ruin, and WWII bric-a-brac, the sirens slept, embracing their sisters and daughters in the gentle current.

The older, revered queens made rules for the middle-aged dames, young huntresses and juvenile pups to follow. The dictum surrounding these early encounters with Man was generally to refrain from surfacing with them afoot. There was no ruling on underwater conduct, however, a mondo loophole the often-reckless huntresses swam right on through. Impish by nature, the mermaids couldn't resist poking dangling surfer extremities. And if a mermaid could resist, if she could wait for a surfer's inevitable pop up, a mermaid could glide in the face of a wave, yank the surfboard out from under and watch a surfer eat hard shit.

Butchie assumed Corky had been pulling his leg about the naked ladies until he was out trying to catch a wave one day and someone (Corky, he guessed) was pulling his actual leg.

He ignored it for a moment and then snapped down, catching a wiry young arm and brushing a bare breast. A bare breast! Butchie stared dumbfounded at a laughing babe. Butchie couldn't have known that her real name is unpronounceable (if you don't have both lungs and a swim bladder) and roughly translates to "exceptionally affable hagfish." He decided he'd call her Peaches on account of her tangled pink mane and sun-ripe flesh.

Butchie guessed they were about the same age—seventeen. He wondered if a honey wild enough to skinny-dip would expect him to go steady and whether he could fit a steady into his already over-crammed semester. No matter. He wanted so badly to neck her, she of the coral hair and sea green eyes.

Peaches cupped his face in her pruned hands. Roughly, she pulled Butchie's head toward her and sniffed his hair, pressing his face to her bare chest. She held him fixed to her, inhaling his wet curls languorously. He was dazed, listening to Peaches' slow heartbeat, his own blood pounding in his ears. He wondered what base this would even count as, nestled between the greatest tits he'd ever seen, debating whether to stay still and let her make a move or whether she was waiting for him to make one. He wanted to wrap his arms around her bare frame and stay there in the bosom of the sea forever. But in a splash, she was gone.

Butchie asked around about Peaches but the beach blanket crowd was no help.

Everyone's guess was that it had been Corky's cousin Frannie. She was the beach's reigning redhead and the strongest swimmer by a mile. And though he wouldn't put it past Frannie to swim in the buff or pull an aquatic prank (she was a notorious pants-er), it wasn't Frannie.

Butchie knew Frannie. And she was cute and all, if you could get past her devotion to her kissing cousin Corky, but Frannie was no Peaches.

Butchie quietly pined throughout the spring. He quit water polo, he quit choraliers. He dreamed of Peaches with the bright pink hair. He mooned over her before he went to sleep and the moment he woke up. He thought of her whenever he took a shower and a couple quick, covert times in the guys' locker room.

Surfing was the only other thing for it. Butchie surfed before school and he surfed after school. He was able to lose himself in the breaks but he was always on the lookout to find his girl. As the weather heated up, more and more surf-curious noobs took to the waves, crowding the lineups. The seasoned surfers called them kooks and gave them flack for spoiling everyone's good time. Guys had to go out of their way to surf around the kooks.

The early summer also brought red tide during the days and glowing waves at night.

Butchie convinced his kook-hating pal Skip to go out surfing with him under a full moon. They howled with joy in the s*ds, painting glowing eddys with their feet and singing to pass the time. Butchie was a serviceable tenor but Skip, unable to suppress his glee club dweebery, lilted in falsetto harmonies, airily surfing on the rise and fall of Butchie's tune.

Peaches floated unseen behind the two, watching their

strong young backs tense and release with the forced flow of breath. As though she'd been hooked on a line, she found herself drifting toward them, transported by the sound. Peaches rested an arm on either longboard, transfixed. Butchie and Skip jerked in unison, catching her silhouette in the bioluminescent glow. A sweet ache dropped in Butchie's stomach. Skip grinned widely and sang on, unfazed by the siren in their midst.

In a tizzy, Butchie dropped into the water, slid his arm around Peaches and kissed her cool mouth, the two of them wrapped in glimmering effervescence. She chuckled lightly, inadvertently clinking Butchie's teeth with hers, then fiercely connected her mouth back to his.

Peaches' enthusiasm and primal beauty more than compensated for her terrible kissing, Butchie reasoned. And as he canoodled with his legs, he realized with some confusion that the surge of bioluminescence rising from below was churned by fins of a long tail. Onward and downward, Butchie resolved, slowly sliding his surveying hand over a scaly rump.

Skip's voice trailed off. Peaches froze. She broke away from tonguing Butchie, holding his hand while gliding over to Skip. Butchie drew Peaches' hand to his heartsick thumping chest. Peaches wrapped her free arm around Skip, pulled him in beside her and put her open mouth to his, letting Skip do the work to give the kiss structure and integrity. Butchie's heart throbbed and fluttered as Peaches' hand pressed on down his torso, gamely disappearing into his trunks.

Mermaids, unlike humans, are voluntary breathers. That doesn't explain Peaches' unorthodox kissing—we'll chalk that up to plain inexperience—but it does shed light on what followed. While the three were deep in one anothers' thrall, off-shore winds picked up. A glowing wave swept over them, sending Butchie hurtling down in a bright blanket of phytoplankton.

Butchie struggled to right himself in the undertow, his already surging chest on the verge of explosion. He kicked and crawled his way to air, found his board, found Skip's board. But no Skip. He called out, he dived down, he swam to the jetty, he swam to the shore. Butchie was half panicked, half seething from the suspicion Skip was off making it with his mermaid.

Butchie stuck around till the early-bird surfers sent him home, promising they'd continue the search for Skip. They ordered him to get some sleep, exchanging worried glances when Butchie rehashed the bits about the sensual and possibly deadly mermaid he'd named Peaches. The surfers reported Skip's disappearance to the coast guard but despite weeks of organized searches, no one ever saw him again.

Peaches couldn't have fathomed that pulling Skip down with her would drown him. She lightly shrugged off his spastic dance followed by unconsciousness since mermaids too take short, unannounced naps. She figured when he awoke, she'd get Skip to do some celestial warbling for the colony. Until she grasped the gravity of her mistake.

It had been an alarmingly lean couple of years for mer-dining. Despite the nearby treatment plant's upgrades, the post-war boom in Los Angeles' population quickly overwhelmed the existing infrastructure. The solution the city settled on was the construction of a pipe five miles out into the ocean. Every month, it pumped out hundreds of millions of pounds of untreated sewage with the plant's lightly treated sludge.

The fish population reeled—went belly-up or cleared on out. Ditto for the crustaceans. Sea worms thrived, but mermaids shuddered and gagged at the thought of eating them. The mermaid queens introduced a "try new things!" campaign that encouraged broadening the colony's fickle palettes. They scrounged for edible human trash which was more abundant in the flotsam by the day. They experimented with new methods of preparing unsavory fare, masking something revolting by drying it out on land and folding it into something more succulent.

But even so, the colony was stressed. These recipes were more time and labor-intensive for the dames, who were already tasked with round-the-clock care of the pups while the huntresses went farther and ever farther afield to find food.

Several huntress mermaids had been scolded for making off with some fatty South Bay Toothfish females. The huntresses said they weren't sorry, whining that the widows had already spawned and weren't much use to anyone. Visibly annoyed at the callow huntresses, the queens warned that poaching any Toothfish set a very dangerous precedent. It might sow distrust among the fertile females, driving them to lay in vulnerable spots outside the den where currents would sweep the larvae out to the open ocean to be eaten by predatory sea life. And then there'd be no more juvenile South Bay Toothfish to grow into mature South Bay Toothfish to fertilize and incubate future mermaids. And who'd be sorry then?

So within moments of Peaches toting her human consort

down to the den in her slipstream, the usual throng of hob-nobbing queens—her grandmother among them—had made their decision. Peaches was horrified as she watched Nonna take an ancient grappling hook and poke a hole in Skip's belly, taking her bloody fill before allowing Peaches' great aunts to drain him like a moonfish.

Despite "try new things!" there were still plenty of repugnant human bits the mermaids passed on to less discerning ocean neighbors. But for the most part, they broke Skip down and ate as much of his flesh as they could stomach, sharing among the colony. It had been a rare honor for Nonna and her direct line—Peaches' ma and sister got the choicest cuts, the tenderest bits. And word got around how easily the prey had been ensnared: just a bit of the old smooch and snag.

So mermaids acquired a taste for man. And scores of surfers gleefully reported rebuffing amorous fish-ladies. Cop a feel and run! Which was pretty funny till it wasn't. The novelty wore off when the surfers realized Dropsy's Chevy hadn't moved for a week and The Sarge's army buddies came around asking all the surfers and beach bums when last they'd last seen him. Then there were the unlucky Standard Oil guys out repairing a section of underwater pipe for the refinery. There were four commercial divers, two mechanics and one guy piloting the small boat who quickly and painfully regretted his decision to jump in and see what the heck was going on down there.

The mermaids were equally thrilled and mystified by the divers' aqualungs and rebreathers. As they did with all the most Glorious Human Tools, they affixed them with lure-laden hooks to the junked-out walls of their den. It was usually here, among the mopey South Bay Toothfish widows, that Peaches sat out the raids, resigning herself to perpetual hunger and solitude. She could make herself ill, thinking about Skip's scavenged body and the reign of terror she'd let loose. There would be no making amends with Butchie, but still she searched for him among the surfers, along the jetty, and as close to the beach as she dared.

Sometimes Peaches' sister Minnie would drift along in her slipstream, amiably asking dumb questions and urging Peaches to cheer up.

Butchie, for his part, stewed in a roiling mess of grief and betrayal. His folks worried. They made him reinstate his non-surfing extracurriculars and when he got his grades up, they bought him a gentlyused Jazzmaster for Christmas. If something good could be borne of the tragedy of Skip, it was the music Butchie started making with Skip's El Segundo High glee club buddies who sang at the vigils, and later on, at the memorials. They called themselves The Hang Ten Men. There were six of them, actually, and save Butchie, not a one of them surfed.

Butchie wrote surf dirges on his guitar—heavy on reverb and lay choral stylings—and Skip's tenor pal Gene countered their weight with buoyant pop arrangements. Gene was good friends with drummer and bassist twin brothers who played in the University High School band, ten swank miles north. The Uni twins knew two crack guitarists, both named Warren. And as luck would have it, the twins' dad was some broadcast honcho with friends in every A&R department worth its salt. That fall, they played the Rendezvous Ballroom and the following year, the Hang Ten Men had bona fide chart hits with their first single "Surf 'Round the Clock" and drum-chant instrumental

B-side "Never! Not! Surfing!"

After the Standard Oil incident and the series of missing surfers, those who ventured into the ocean took to arming themselves. Knives were a popular option but limited in their use, best for defensive close-combat. There were a lucky few with access to harpoon guns. Some surfers made spears and practiced chucking them on the beach, other guys paddled out with pistols or rifles or the occasional grenade resting on their boards. Mermaid huntresses are a hardy bunch and the surfers largely missed. Even so, the dames became grievously skilled at patching their daughters up with bone needles and stitches of shark-gut.

At dusk one windy day, Peaches surfaced to do her rounds, managing to give her sister the slip while she scanned for Butchie. Out toward the jetty, a tune faintly reminiscent of Butchie and Skip's pricked her ears. Only this was five voices singing about sun worship and beach babes in chromatic harmony. Entranced, Peaches found herself shimmying up the jetty to the locus of the sublime strains. Curiously, it came not from men but from a Glorious Human Tool—a freshly pressed 45 spinning around Frannie's portable record player. It wasn't Butchie or any of the Hang Ten Men but fellow local surf band the Banzai Brothers with their breakout single, "Surfin' Turf." Peaches hoisted herself up the rocky incline in a blind frenzy, clambering toward the sound. As a last strum sustained and faded, Peaches' vision tingled and sharpened. She found herself stuck on the jetty, bewildered, being regarded by a red-headed huntress with human legs.

Frannie gently extended an arm to Peaches. Frannie was not

of the sea, Peaches concluded. Her hair was more copper than pink and she covered herself modestly with a bikini. There was, however, something she recognized and trusted in Frannie's sweet face. Peaches let Frannie embrace her, helping her tail-first back down the slope until Peaches was torso-deep. Peaches reached for Frannie, giving her a careful kiss, wary not to drag Frannie underwater. Frannie smiled to herself, scampered back to her blanket and returned moments later. She unwrapped Corky's tuna fish sandwich, offering it to Peaches. Peaches blithely accepted, dunked the sandwich in the saltwater and did some combination of mastication, regurgitation and bonus digestion that made Frannie nearly lose her own lunch.

A sharp bleat pierced the air. Peaches recognized it reflexively, hurtling herself into the foam. Frannie hesitated before throwing her board in and pounding after.

Peaches found her sister Minnie viciously grappling with a brawny surfer. Minnie was bleeding from her gut, floundering, attempting to wrest a large knife from Corky's grip. Peaches lunged at Corky, pummeling and clawing and trying in vain to extricate her shrieking sister.

Corky managed to swipe both mermaids before Frannie reached him, using her body as a buffer. She tore him off the huntresses and embraced Corky fiercely, restraining his arms until they relaxed. Corky buried his head in Frannie's neck and she kissed his wet hair. She sorrowfully watched the mermaids dip down and vanish in a dark bloom.

Peaches spirited Minnie to their Mama and Nonna—Peaches had little more than a scratch but Minnie was failing, her insides deeply gashed, her inky blood unstaunchable. Mama sewed and Peaches applied pressure nevertheless. Nonna laid Minnie's head on her scaly lap, she stroked her billowing hair, she watched with sinking certainty as the pup she raised went still and silent.

Minnie hadn't been the colony's only casualty—over the course of the spring, scores of mermaids were mortally wounded in skirmishes with the surfers. Porkchop single-handedly dispatched a handful of huntresses with his ex-frogman dad's harpoon gun. KA-BAR clenched between his teeth, Da Mute silently snuck up behind two arguing, oblivious queens. A kook named Lucky threw a grenade into a school of dames teaching pups to breathe above water.

Man was not the kissy lunk they'd reckoned he was. No, he could very easily be the death of their colony. Convinced that eradicating the surfer problem would end all their woes, the clan started hunting for blood sport. The queens mandated a surfer slaughter a day with the most gruesome, agitprop staging the colony could muster. There were sun-bleached surfer heads on spikes, planted deep in the damp sand. There were surfing skeletons that washed ashore, still wearing their baggies, their bones picked clean. There was the broken board and the pile of guts formerly known as Corky.

Peaches absented herself to the colony's loud displeasure. She didn't want revenge, she wanted to hole up in the den and bear the full weight of her guilt and sorrow. She found there was a light blip in her grief when Peaches surrounded herself with the Toothfish males. She could ignore her pain wiling away the day in their dopey calm. The Toothfish males were so refreshingly limited in their desires. They would ingest anything that came their way and break wind like it was going out of style. Some mermaids posited that South Bay Toothfish used these high-pitched gassy expulsions to communicate with one another but Peaches thought that was giving the Toothfish far too much credit. Toothfish weren't the cleverest fish in the sea but at least the males were diverting, if flatulent company.

The females, conversely, were downright insufferable. They were poky and nervous, messy and helpless. Peaches watched day in and day out as they loafed on the den's seabed, mooching off the colony's limited resources, crapping where they ate. Peaches figured she was probably doing everyone a favor when, every couple days, out of sight from the den, she furtively nicked and wolfed down the reigning worst widow Toothfish.

Peaches understood this act was beyond verboten but her body was readying for reproduction, begging her for animal protein. In fact, she was but one of many anemic, similarly transgressing mermaids. What were they supposed to do? Eating worms was out of the question and they weren't about to eat surfer beef, the only meat the huntresses were bagging of late. If the huntresses were too malnourished to lay eggs, there wouldn't be any point to keeping the South Bay Toothfish around, right? And anyway, Peaches suspected South Bay Toothfish were far too thick to be anything but impervious to the snatchings.

One day, Peaches' body led her in an unfamiliar dance. The biggest, strongest South Bay Toothfish male dug her a tribute of a nest and Peaches surprised herself by serenely laying four pearly eggs. The alpha South Bay Toothfish fertilized them and delicately collected the eggs for mouthbrooding alongside his fellow Toothfish papa friends in the winter months to come.

Peaches resolved to clean up her act in anticipation of her impending motherhood. As the sun set on her huntress years, she would become an engaged, rule-abiding dame spending her days blithely doing the domestic work of the den.

It was around this time Peaches heard murmurings around the colony about the trance-inducing, sunny sounds the surfers could produce. Peaches realized she wasn't the only one held in thrall when she heard those torrid rhythms, the syrupy harmonies, the thick reverb that made her ache. Several mermaids described finding themselves beached, disoriented, weeping and laughing and utterly vulnerable as the last hypnotic chords issued from a Glorious Human Tool. They'd been lucky to wiggle themselves back into the tide unnoticed. Others, they guessed, had been less lucky.

The wisest queens wondered: Did man know he had this power? And if he didn't yet know, could they prevent him from finding out?

But more pressing still was the matter of the dwindling food supply. Even a surfer a day wasn't cutting it; the colony was wan and the pups whimpered with hungry bellies in their sleep. The constraints of the academic calendar and the wintry weather limited the availability of surfers. The easy pickings were gone and the guys toughing it out there in the cold contested waters were wiley, armed and dangerous.

Peaches overheard the queens hotly debate the risks and merits of moving the colony.

Was it certain death to go? Or stay? They were unsure if there were any suitable habitats within weeks of swimming distance, unsure of new predators or available prey, unsure if there were other populations of South Bay Toothfish willing to do the mermaids' reproductive bidding. Perhaps their current South Bay Toothfish friends would be willing to pick up and move in tow?

But in the end, with their heady mix of gall and invention, the surfers won out. As an old mermaid adage goes: Though the ocean is vast, men rule the day. They blow mud in the sea, then they ride on the waves.

To dedicate a new name and matching plaque for the beach, the locals put together a celebratory bonfire cookout and concert. A popular radio station erected and electrified a stage on the sand with The Hang Ten Men, the Banzai Brothers, the Surflords, the Sonnys, Doodle & Bruce, and Wahini Tina all slated to play. As the sun went down that eventide, it was maybe ten minutes into the Hang Ten Men's set when the bloodbath commenced.

Deep on the seafloor, the dames made an unthinkable discovery: The shit-brain South Bay Toothfish males broke with mouthbrooding protocol and swallowed all of the mermaid eggs. Evidently, they had indeed noticed the shriveling female population, apoplectically pooping their displeasure to one another. It was coordinated spite and not sheer stupidity, the dames reflected between sobs. They conveyed the heavy news to the queens, who sent the huntresses out in packs to round up and punish the errant South Bay Toothfish males, maybe—with any luck—rescuing any undigested mermaid eggs in the process.

In a corona of tiki torch light, Butchie and the Hang Ten Men began their set with an a capella ballad to the sun. They closed their eyes and wove their vocal strands into a delicate harmony.

As the boozy beach crowd jockeyed for stage-front position, a low groan issued from the sea. Panic spread through the crowd, everyone straining to see what was going down.

Butchie and the Hang Ten Men's singing had lured dozens of mermaids to come thrashing in the surf. The huntresses were ignoring their Toothfish-tracking directive, moaning and writhing in an enrapt group army crawl up the sand. Sonically overwhelmed, they were beaching themselves. The mermaids clawed frantically as if they could scale the wall of sound.

Breathless at the opportunity, a bunch of surf guys grabbed their guns and machetes. Butchie and the Hang Ten Men's two guitarists named Warren added their wet reverb to the choral sun ballad. As an accelerating drum line picked up steam and as the beach bunnies broke into their frenzied Watusi, the surfers shot and hacked their way through the spellbound sirens.

Butchie caught his bandmates' eyes. He could tell they were sickened, considering whether to dive off the stage to interrupt the massacre. Because they weren't surfers. Because they hadn't been attacked and bullied, because they weren't out with Skip that awful glow-in-the dark night and because it wasn't their buddy Corky who'd been reduced to a staring pile of viscera. Gunshot reports, pulpy thwacking, and excruciating wailing in the waves drowned out the Hang Ten Men's cover of "Surf If You Got It."

Gene stopped singing and staggered to his feet, lifting his hands off the organ's keys. Equally appalled, the twins went silent. The Warrens were too shocked to move let alone sing or strum. The music died with a sharp feedback screech. The mermaids stirred from their trance. One sunk her teeth deep into Lucky's ankle, rupturing his Achilles tendon before Rats riddled her with bullets. Two mermaids grabbed Doodle's legs, a third pulled him down, a fourth snatched his machete and off went his head.

Butchie tried in vain to restart "Surf If You Got It." The Hang Ten Men stared in shock at the nightmare in the waves. Butchie shuddered at the grisly mass of mermaids in the shallow water but played on. Was Peaches in there? He didn't know, he tried not to care.

Some jerk threw a beer can at the stage, grazing the taller Warren's head. Butchie scanned the angry crowd. "Play, you nitwits!" a beach bunny shouted. A preppy in the front row had detached a tiki torch and was brandishing it too close to the rattan stage siding for Butchie's comfort. He exhorted his band to play. "For Skip, dammit! Strike it up for Skip!" Gene played a couple chords, leaned over and retched.

Just then, all four drunken Surflords jumped on stage. They struck up their hit single, "SUN SUN SUN SUN FUN FUN FUN FUN" and Butchie joined in, following the chord changes at a slight lag, harmonizing where he could. The three Banzai Brothers mounted the crowded stage and joined in, making it an eight-part harmony, perfectly blending their fraternal voices.

Wahini Tina climbed on up, shimmying barefoot with her Stratocaster, adding a ninth voice on the very top. Buoyed by sheer harmonic power, Butchie's fellow Hang Ten Men got their voices back and resumed playing their respective instruments. Butchie nodded and gestured pointedly, more or less conducting the Hang Ten Men, the Surflords, the Banzai Brothers and Wahini Tina. They correctly read his signals to repeat the bridge before circling back to three—no, four—encore choruses and right on into an extended version of "Surfing Baby."

The mermaids convulsed and went still in ecstatic torpor, their eyes welled from the transcendent melody. It was in this state that they died, pinioned by the sound, slaughtered whole-sale in a matter of minutes.

When the last of the mermaids lay motionless, The Hang Ten Men chugged a celebratory six-pack apiece, priming them-selves for the unpleasant task at hand. They rooted through the combined sights and smells of both fish market and abattoir, dragging the least cumbersome pulp—arms mostly—to the nearest beach bonfire. Only the Hang Ten Men were plumb tuckered out by the music and the melee and were quickly grasp-ing that mermaid remains are surprisingly heavy. Also, the beers had just barely wet their respective whistles.

Screw it, let's get shit-faced, they agreed. The tide was on the rise and within the hour, the scores of broken huntresses' bodies had been washed back to sea.

Frannie sat at that nearest bonfire, her face hot and numb. She didn't think about Corky and the others nor Peaches and her kind. Absorbed by the popping consumption of wet mer-maid flesh and the not-unpleasant smell of crackling fat, she watched the licking flames with eyes unfocused.

Peaches and her huntress posse returned from their rescue mission in a dark cloud of fish blood. They'd successfully extracted one intact egg from the belly of the alpha male Toothfish before skewering him and his whole school. And on their way back to the den, they'd found what was left of their sister huntresses and wept. They were beyond saving so the huntresses left their mangled bodies to the waves.

Tomorrow the surviving mermaids would move their colony down the coast, bleary-eyed and gravely unsure of their fate. But tonight, after so much deprivation, after all the guilt and grieving, the mermaids would feast. They would toast their fallen sisters, they would draw their untroubled pups close. They would revel together, devouring every last bit of every last larval, juvenile and adult South Bay Toothfish in the sea.

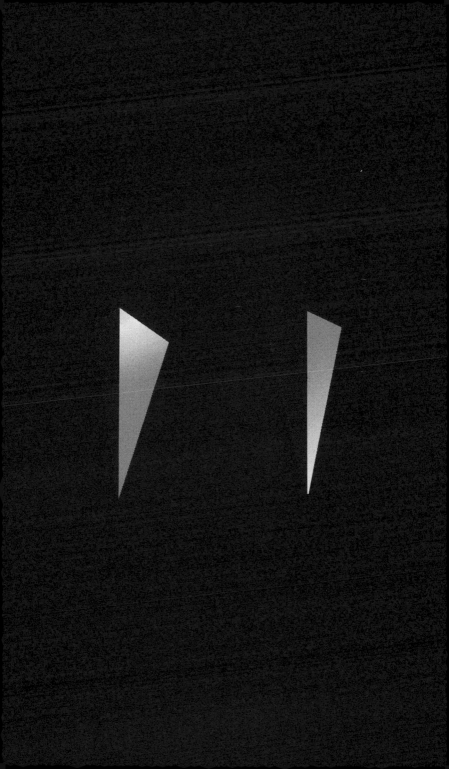

Nate Hillyer

SEAN MADIGAN HOEN

God of Thunder

They sent me alone to give Craig his pills, as I was the only one
on speaking terms with him, the only one of us now who'd dare
breach the doorway of the mobile home in which he lived with a
woman named Sheila. Craig's mother, of all people, put me up
to it. Craig's brother, Sean, was my best friend and I'd known
him and Craig since I was six or so. Craig was seven years older.
Which meant that by this time, the time of my pharmaceutical
delivery, he was about nineteen, because I specifically recall
being twelve, the exact age I was when Ms. Fowery began
buying Sean and me beer. I remember this because when Ms.
Fowery told me I was the one, I'd said to her for the first time,
"Buy me a forty, and I'll do it."

That became my response to anything she'd ask of me that
year, and for a few to come: "Buy me a forty."

I hadn't seen Craig since a day several months earlier, in
summer, when he pulled up the Fowerys' driveway in a rusted
blue Mustang riddled with bullet holes. It was Sheila's car. Her

ex-boyfriend had shot it up in one night, a thing Craig seemed vaguely proud of, especially when, upon being asked about the damage, he told us, "I'm gonna stick that gun up his asshole," which was about as verbal as Craig could be. Actually that might not be true. Of Sheila he'd said, "She's not black, she's ebony," which all these years later seems like a poetic, post-coital thing Sheila must have whispered to him. Ebony: It seemed profound to me at the time. We were what I'd many years later, in a bar somewhere in California, hear someone refer to as "dirty white boys." To date a black woman was exotic to us, then, at that age, in exurbs of the Midwest—Craig had been the portrayer of so many exotic things over the years, dope and liquor and heavy metal and horror films—but this particular story has nothing to do with race as far as I know. Sheila's previous boyfriend, the one who shot up the car, was another dirty white boy named Neil Phillips—a psycho about whom we'd heard terrible things—and Craig had taken Neil's spot in Sheila's trailer, and it seemed very likely that none of this was over, the bullet holes only the beginning.

Not long after that Craig disappeared, or stopped coming around, which meant he wasn't picking up his meds from Ms. Fowery, who'd had them prescribed for herself so that the insurance from her secretarial job would cover the pills. What these pills were, I have no idea. Lithium, possibly. Or something very strong. Because without them Craig was mentally deranged. Something had happened to him as a boy—I sort of knew this, and knew it was sexual, but I didn't know quite what, exactly, had happened. People didn't talk then like they would later, didn't confess things like this to the world. It was a secret that wasn't a secret, at least not to me.

"You can get through to him," said Ms. Fowery. "Talk about heavy metal with him, and try to get him to take one of the pills, in front of you, he always liked you..."

Craig had lashed his mother with a garden hose when she'd gone by the trailer; a superficial lashing, I believe, as he'd struck out only at her calves, but still... He'd been calling the house and telling Sean he was a "greasy little hog," making fun of his weight issues and threatening to tie him up and feed him to death. He'd completely snapped. His friends were losers who couldn't be bothered with him. Sean and Craig had different fathers, neither of whom were anywhere near the picture.

Does it pain me now, years later, to recall my humble beginnings?

It truly does.

Especially things like my visions of Ms. Fowery walking out of Safeway with two forties of Molson Ice in a brown paper sack, boarding her Ford Tempo, saying, "I'll drop you off a block away and you just walk up to the door and pound on it until he answers."

The Warwick Village Mobile Home Park was a system of dirt roads and geometrically arranged trailers. I'd passed it many times on my bicycle, always pedaling a little faster as I neared. Darkness resonated from the place, no matter the hour. You'd look down one of the dirt roads and see filthy people in their underwear, smoking, drinking from plastic cups, kicking the dirt—they always seemed to be doing the same things—looking mean. Even the kids, who we never saw in school, despite The Warwick being within city limits.

Ms. Fowery did as she'd said and dropped me off a block away in a 7-Eleven parking lot.

"Make sure he takes it in front of you, Blondie…" she'd said, because my name is also Sean and her son and I were distinguished by our weight and hair color. Despite Sean's obesity people called me "Big Sean," because I was a year older, while others knew us as "Skinny Sean" and "Fat Sean," or "Blondie" and "Brown." Fat Sean was in the backseat weeping, possibly about food, which was how he always got what he wanted—or I might be confused, remembering him as a child rather than a young boy of eleven—but he was there, in the backseat, when they dropped me off.

"Tell Craig to fuck off and die," he said, though he didn't mean that.

They both wanted me to succeed.

I walked the quick block to the Warwick and turned down the first dirt road, looking for trailer number sixty-four. Dirty snow still lined the edges of the road, as the entire area was covered by a canopy of trees and received no sunlight—that might have been the last snow to melt in all of Dearborn Heights. The pill bottle was in the front pocket of my jeans. I didn't think to look at it.

I found Trailer sixty-four. It was battered, with weeds and vines having attached themselves to its dented aluminum siding, its Plexiglas windows insulated by sheets of cardboard. A cheap, movable set of plastic steps led up to the door. There were beer cans on each step and an ashtray atop the small landing. It had a rusty handrail. When I reached the door, I knocked hard, like Ms. Fowery told me to.

At first I heard nothing.

Then I heard someone, a man, singing a melody I knew but couldn't place.

Ba-dah-dah-dah... and-bah-dah-dah-dah.

Have you ever known you could just walk into someplace, that something awaited you and only you on the other side of a door? That you were supposed to enter a certain place at a certain time to view a scene meant only for the annals of your private memory? Like your own movie, the one of your life— you're about to be given a crucial scene?

I turned the knob and the door opened.

I walked inside, into a meager kitchen in which Craig was sitting at a table, smearing white corpse paint all over his face and singing.

When he saw me he cut off the melody and turned his head slowly toward me, away from whatever abyss he'd been staring off into. It was the first time I'd seen pure madness, felt snagged in the whorling vortex of the insane. The look in his eyes told me everything. The pupils were huge, dilated in a way that made them account for more space than the rest of his features combined—they filled the kitchen. He was staring through me.

"I have your pills," I told him.

His face was almost completely white, and once he dipped his hand into the makeup jar again and performed another application, it was completely white. His crazy eyes fluttered as he did this, the eyelids white and cracked. Then he started in with the black paint, meticulous now, using just a finger as if it were a very fine pen. Since he had no mirror, he was drawing his mask from memory.

"You're supposed to take your pills, Craig," I told him. "They'll make you feel better."

"I am the God of Thunder," he told me.

Then it all—the melody and the makeup—came together: He'd been singing a song by the band Kiss and was painting himself up like one of the members, which one I couldn't be sure, the spaceman or the cat man or the star child or the monster? I recalled that, when off his meds, Craig often regressed to the Kiss fandom of his boyhood...

"I am the God of Thunder," he said again.

"And rock and roll..." I sang back to him, which was how the lyric went—he'd taught me the song when I was very young, six or seven years old.

We began singing together:

God of Thunder/And rock n' ro-oh-oll

The spell you're under/Will slowly rob you of your virgin soul

And each time we sang this last line, about robbing one of their virgin soul, he reached out the index finger of his free hand and used it to motion for me to come closer, his other hand still attending to his makeup...and each time we sang I took another step, his giant eyes hungry for something, closer and closer, the pills rattling in my pocket as my leg began to shake, as his large hand reached for me, closer now, his mask coming finally into view: He was becoming the monster, the one who spit blood, flicked his tongue, robbed youth of their souls, whose own soul had been robbed from his youth...

God of Thunder/And rock n' ro-oh-oll
...and I took another step and did not turn away.

BENJAMIN SMART

Asylum

A person's life belongs only to them, and they have the right to end it should they wish. Suicide is the most basic right of all. Freedom is self-ownership. If someone can force you to live, you do not own yourself: You belong to them.

Of course, this isn't a healthy mindset to have. Especially if it's your job to talk people out of it.

I worked as an At-Home Mental Health Coordinator for the William Durant Psychiatric Hospital in the City. I responded to calls from patients with a history of suicidal or otherwise self-harming behavior. I would come to their residence, talk with them, try to deescalate the situation. If I deemed it necessary, I'd see to it that they were placed under a seventy-two-hour psychiatric hold.

The job was all right. Usually the patients were calm, and they'd come out of the situation in a better mood than they went into it.

But there were a few cases that bothered me.

One of the first took me to a neighborhood just south of Old Town, where the streets were rough with potholes and the tenant buildings were dilapidated, slouching shells of what they used to be.

The address I'd been called to was an apartment building whose rooms were rented out a week at a time. In the lobby was a caged-in front desk whose attendant was absent. I found my way to the third floor and walked down a hallway laid all the way with worn red carpet. A woman with dark mascara and leggings eyed me as I passed.

I felt conspicuous, and was relieved when I found the right door. Its eyehole had been broken or removed, was now simply clotted with a rolled-up brown paper towel. I knocked three times.

"Come in," a low, somber voice said from inside.

The door jammed when I turned the knob, then rattled as I pushed it open. Inside was a morbidly large woman sitting on the bed's edge, wiping her eyes. She had short hair dyed black, and she wore a Dallas Cowboys shirt as a gown.

The smell was horrific. Something I couldn't identify was decomposing. From top to bottom the shelves and counters and dressers were stacked with take-out bags, dishes half-alive with maggots, and each visible piece of furniture and linen was stained implacably brown.

I had a strong urge to gag, run out and catch my breath. But instead I smiled.

"Heather," I said, moving toward the room's center. "I'm Olivia. I'm here about the call you made. I'd like to chat with you for a bit."

"Okay." She was stoic, hadn't glanced at me since I'd come in.

Two months earlier, according to her file, she'd been released from William Durant for repeated self-harming behavior and suicidal ideation.

I proceeded to ask her all the basic questions a little quicker than usual due to my queasiness: How long had she been having these thoughts? Did she have a plan to end her life? How far had she gone to prepare for it? What were her plans if I left her alone? If she decided against it, what were her plans for the next few days?

We talked for a while. Not about anything specific, the little things.

"You remind me of myself," she said a few minutes into our talk.

"And why's that?"

"Because you're optimistic, the way I used to be." She paused. "Would you hand me those cigarettes?"

On the coffee table near me was a pack of Turkish Royals. I handed it to her, and she lit one, continued speaking:

"I wasn't always like this." She placed a hand beneath her elbow. "I used to be a runner, cross country geek. Used to run six miles each day before school. I was just a skinny little thing then. You wouldn't of recognized me. That was till about four years ago. I'd just moved here, had taken to running those trails around Butler Lake 'cause all the traffic in the city drove me up the wall. And plus I liked being alone out there, far away from everyone, free and all. Anyway, one day I was running and I came up on a rocky part of the trail, down in a sort of valley, beside a creek, when I step on a loose rock and stumble and fall down into it. Now, I didn't feel it at first. But, when I tried to get up, it felt like the bones in my leg were gonna pop right out, and it just hurt like I thought nothing could.

"I was about four miles out in a pretty isolated part of the trail, but I figure someone will come along sooner or later. But a good amount of time passes, and my leg's hurting worse, and it's starting to get dark and still nobody's come. So I start screaming and hollering and carrying on, but I guess no one heard me. I'm out there all alone all night, and it's October, late October, when it starts getting real cold at night. Seems like every part of me goes numb but my leg, which just hurts to high heaven. So I'm out there all night by myself, scared to death no one will ever find me.

"But eventually someone does, came across me about eleven the next morning. I heard their footsteps and just started screaming, and they take a peek over the ridge, and there I am. They told whoever they needed to, and about an hour and a half later I'm being carried out of there. That was the first time I'd ever had morphine or anything like that, gave it to me as soon as they found me. I just remember what a relief it was. All my pain, all my fear, my regret, washed away with a single needle. I think I slept for a day, I was so tired.

"Now the doctors did the best they could, but my kneecap and pretty much the entire upper half of my tibia and fibula were shattered. They can only fix you to a certain point. After the surgery I hurt worse than when it happened. They sent some Oxycotin home with me, said the pain should subside after a while. But it never did, and it's been four years now. Till this day it feels like my leg's gonna snap in two if I stand on it. They used to give me Oxycotin for it. But all they can do for that kind of pain is give you more pills. And I liked those too much. Eventually, I started takin' too many, did dumb, stupid stuff to get more.

"But I'm off those now, state made sure of that. Now it just hurts. All the time. There's no end to it. All I have is pain. It's been with me so long that it seems like a part of me. I'm not ever going to escape it, and I've come to live with that."

Her words were disconnected from the rest of her. They were more like a speech she'd rehearsed, trying to make me believe something. But, as she lit another cigarette and stared at me with bitterness and hatred, I couldn't figure out what that was.

"So if you've accepted it, then why am I here?"

"Accepting it and living with it are two different things. One's so much easier than the other. Pain doesn't change, no matter how hard you try and understand it."

She ashed her cigarette, began massaging her leg. The skin of it was as mangled and discolored as that of a burn victim.

"You know," she began, almost in a whisper, forcing me to come closer, "that night in the forest was pretty strange. I don't think I've ever told anyone. I don't know why that is."

She didn't seem aware of my presence, talking to herself.

"As I was lying there in the creek, cold, shivering, in pain, I could've sworn I heard someone laughing. At first I tried yelling out, catch their attention. But no one hollered back, no one came, but that laughing never stopped. It was just quiet enough to hear it, you know? And it was so quiet, and the laughter was so faint, that I wasn't sure I'd heard it at all. And then, in the early-morning hours, one or two a.m., just as the moon was coming out enough to see a little bit, I saw someone standing on the ridge in the distance. I couldn't make out anything about them except that they were there. It was like someone had taken the space of where a person should be and filled it with blackness. Then the laughter died off, and that voice that'd been laughing said a song or poem or something. It was just as quiet as the laughter, I could barely hear it, but I made out the words just fine. Then it was gone, the laughter and all."

She sat there silently. Suddenly I realized that she'd gone pale, had cold sweat glistening on her forehead.

"Heather? Are you feeling okay?"

She said nothing, passed over my question with a smile.

"Did you take something?"

I moved over to her, examined her eyes. They were yellow.

"What did you take?"

She was smilingly brightly now, and she stared into me with this smile and recited:

"I shall not want my death so soon.
For even Asylum takes of the world for being,
Even Asylum goes mad with winter, summer, autumn and spring.
And my children will change into men."

The words took me out of myself. She'd whispered them barely loud enough for me to hear, yet my ears rang afterward, and her voice echoed in my head.

I didn't fully remember where I was until Heather fell over, convulsing. By the time I'd reached her, rolled her onto her side, I was already on an emergency line.

"What did you take?"

Her breath was shallow, and her pupils wandered all over the place. I stood up, scanned the room. Beside the bed were two bottles of extra-strength Tylenol. I picked them up. They were empty.

I held the bottles down before her face.

"When did you take these?"

From me to the bottles her eyes wavered, still convulsing, her breath shortening.

"I'm sorry," she said, beginning to cry. "I took them this morning. I'm sorry. I shouldn't have called you out here. I just didn't want to be alone...I didn't want to be alone..."

I told the operator we had an acetaminophen overdose.

An acetaminophen overdose is a painful way to go. There isn't anything they can do beyond a certain point. Your liver becomes overloaded and fails. Then all the toxins and waste it was filtering build up in your body, and your other organs follow. Usually the kidneys go first, followed by the spleen and pancreas. Your unfiltered blood becomes more and more acidic as it circulates, eating away at your cardiovascular tissue until your heart gives out, too.

But this takes days to happen. Meanwhile, you're fully aware your insides are turning to mush, and so are the doctors, and so is your family, but the only thing that'll save you at this point is a new liver. And people wait years for one of those.

I rode with her in the ambulance, held her hand as the EMTs began an IV, gave her fluids. All I could do was hold her hand. The whole thing seemed helpless. All the king's men couldn't put her back together. They'd admit her and give her a wristband and a room and maybe even a little medication to make her comfortable, and a few days later she'd be dead.

And I was aware of all this as held her hand, as she slipped in and out of consciousness, groaning. Once or twice she tried to say something, and I did my very best to make sense of it. I really did. I lowered my ear and even closed my eyes to focus. But I'd already heard it.

"...even Asylum takes of the world for being,
Even Asylum goes mad with winter, summer, autumn and spring..."

I wanted so badly to understand. She was in so much pain, and it must've agonized her to even whisper. And it would've been easier to have said nothing, to shut the world out until the Dilaudid kicked in, spend her final waking hours in a haze, drifting in and out. But whatever she was trying to tell me was too important to be lost with her. And its meaning and repercussions lurked somewhere within the poem she kept reciting.

They separated us at the hospital. By then the Dilaudid had come on, and in the relief of it she was more dead than alive.

One of the nurses drove me to get my car when her shift ended. The doctors told me they'd try to keep her in an opiate-induced coma for the time she had left.

Three days later I read in a newspaper that she had died.

We moved into the city to further our professional careers, my husband and I. He took a job at Niacyclia Co., and we settled into one of those stone-fenced communities not far from downtown. It was a nice neighborhood in a good school district, which was important. Our daughter, Elaine, had been born only a few months prior. I took care of her in the morning while Marshall was at work, and he returned the favor in the evenings.

Cities have always made me nervous. So many people so close together, a million distinct lives bunched into a circle five miles wide. I've always liked my space. When I was a kid, at my parents' house in the country, I would sometimes walk to the end of our drive and stand in the road a long time. Nobody'd pass for hours on those old rock roads, and the only sounds were the bullfrogs and the locusts groaning in the tall grass. The city would be a distant glow on the horizon; the wind would blow in softly from the west. And above me an arm of the Milky Way would cut across the sky, a gash of glowing dead sand, and a warm sort loneliness would flow through me.

But the stars never came out in the City. Too many lights. It was an organism with a million different parts with a million different functions. It sucked you into itself, put pressure on you.

That's when I first started waking up early. Usually I slept in until nine or ten, even eleven if I felt like it. Working second shift allows that sort of thing. But I always woke up way before that in the city, two or three in the morning, and I could never fall back asleep. I didn't wake up peacefully, either. Always coming to with a jolt, a strange restlessness growing. But I could never remember what I'd been dreaming of, if I'd been dreaming at all.

On nights like that, as I laid tensely in bed, trying hard to fall back asleep, I began to slip out of the room and stand before our kitchen's sliding-glass door and stare out across the backyard. Sometimes, when she needed to be fed or changed or simply held, I would gently take my daughter from her crib and into the kitchen and rock her silently in the night.

I don't know why I did this. Maybe I knew that one day I'd have to let her out into the nameless streets of the city. Whatever it was made me restless, and I'd rock her with greater and greater intensity until she woke up and cried. Then I'd catch myself, and soothe her back to sleep.

But I wouldn't put her back in her crib. Still I'd stand there by the sliding-glass door, musing over that starless and dying city, rocking, rocking.

Sometimes I would stand there with her in my arms until morning.

The incident with Heather stuck with me, as did that little poem she recited. For reasons I'm still not able to discern, I scribbled it down on a notebook page and tore it out. Maybe I just didn't want to forget it. But I was so secretive about it, tucked it way in the back of my nightstand drawer so no one would find it.

The call that would eventually lead me to leave my job introduced me to a young man named Brian.

Brian lived alone in a tiny house within an old housing project near the river. He was twenty-four years old and a diagnosed schizophrenic.

It was a cold fall day when I first met him, and the sky was blanketed with heavy gray clouds. From my parked car I spent a few minutes studying his yard: composed almost entirely of bare dirt, littered with spots of brown grass and displaying countless humanoid statues of rusted metal. Some posed as pedestrians, other as graceful Olympians, but they each possessed a wispy, anorexic quality, their ill-fitting clothes tattered and torn, carrying a sense of decomposition, something dead walking.

I followed a slender path weaved through them to the door, knocked.

A sallow young man appeared behind it. He was tall, lanky, had wiry blond hair and swollen purple bags beneath his eyes. The acrid smell of tobacco smoke drifted out.

"Brian?"

"Yeah?" He stood half behind the door, leaning into it.

"My name's Olivia. I'm with the William Durant psychiatric center." I shook his hand. "I'm here about the call you made."

"That was quick."

"Well, this is urgent. Can I come in?"

"Yeah sure." He opened the door all the way. "Watch your step. Sorry it's such a mess."

"Oh, I've seen worse. Believe me, no worries." I shut the door behind me.

The inside was dark. Clothes and bins and boxes covered

the floor, and I was careful not to trip over them as my eyes adjusted. Leaned against the wall in stacks were canvases of dark, abstract images. In the corners stood a couple of rustic statues. I couldn't tell if they were finished.

The kitchen was relatively clean: sink free of dishes, surfaces bare.

"Want some coffee?"

"Sure," I said, examining the windows, each covered up and down with tinfoil, letting in only a sliver of light toward the edge, giving the whole place a dirty yellow hue.

From a Thermos he poured coffee into a mug and handed it to me. I held it with two hands. The liquid was steaming and thick and gave off a sour smell. I sipped tentatively; it was bitter.

"Do you have any creamer or sugar or something like that?"

"Oh, is it too strong?"

"It has a little kick."

"Sorry. I don't have people over often. I forget how strong I make it. I just keep making it stronger and stronger so it keeps working. Hang on." He rummaged through a few cupboards. "I don't think I have any creamer or sugar. Would milk work?"

I nodded, and he retrieved a half gallon from the fridge and handed it to me. The coffee turned brown and cloudy as I poured. I sipped it again. It was cooler and still fairly bitter, but drinkable.

"Thank you." I returned the milk to the fridge, moved over to the table. "Is it okay if we have a seat and talk in here?"

"You can sit. I'll stand. I get restless."

I sat down and asked, casually, "What's this tinfoil on your windows?"

"Oh, the 911 operator told me to do that."

"The 911 operator told you to do that?"

"Yeah," he smiled, a little red in the cheeks. "Sometimes I get a little paranoid at night, usually at night. I think, you know, there's someone outside watching me. Sometimes I hear knocking, whispering, laughing, stuff like that. I can usually keep a clear head, remind myself what's going on. But when it's four a.m. and it's been happening all night and I'm trying to sleep, well, you know, it gets to me. Sometimes I call 911. They used to send a patrol car out here when it first started. But then they learned who I was, what I had, and now they try to 'resolve' it over the phone. I must've been calling in more than I thought, must've gotten on someone's nerves because the other night they told me to put tinfoil on the windows. Or maybe they were trying to humor me. I don't know. But," he chuckled, "it kind of works, funny enough. I used to see shadow people outside sometimes. Just silhouettes, stuff like that. Pretty startling. And now I can't look out the windows, so I can't see those anymore. I think it's helping with the voices and laughing and stuff, too. You know, the auditory hallucinations. But maybe that's just a placebo or whatever." He sipped his coffee. "Plus I like it dark in here."

"What medication are you taking?"

"Zyprexa."

"When did you begin taking that?"

"In college."

"So you've been on that for about five or six years now? Do you think it's working?"

"I think so. I mean, I'm still hearing things. I can still be pretty irrational. But I've gone off it a few times, and it's like I leave the planet when I don't take it. I don't really have more hallucinations. I've never experienced complete psychosis. It's other stuff. People think schizophrenia is all hearing stuff and seeing things and thinking people are out to get you. But that's not the worst part. When I've gone off my medication, it's like I'm a goldfish or something. I don't know if I can explain it. You know how people think, right? They see things, hear things, their senses pick up information, but they're able to take what they experience in accordance to what they already know. They can make sense of the world. It's not like that with me. I take everything at face value. The smallest similarities between two things will completely warp my perception."

He began speaking faster, saying so much so quickly, not glancing once toward me as he talked, not stopping for a moment to see if I understood because he didn't want to be understood. He wanted to be listened to.

"It's like an aquarium. We're supposed to see aquariums from a distance behind a glass. That way it's clear to us; we can see all the different fish, their different sizes and colors, the filter, the decorative little boat on the bottom. We can see it all separately, make sense of it. But schizophrenics are inside the aquarium. They see everything from right there in the center of it. And it's blurry and intense and confusing. Everything happens so quickly and with such potency that we can't make sense of it, and everything we know becomes impossible to grasp. That's the hardest part: the confusion."

"Disorganized thinking."

"Yeah." He put out his cigarette, began rubbing his hands together. "That's what the doctors call it. It sounds something like ADD when they use that name."

I'd listened closely as he spoke, nodding silently. "Are you seeing a psychiatrist, Brian?"

"Twice a month, to check up on my medication." He stirred and downed the rest of his coffee, poured another cup.

"What do you talk about?"

"My symptoms, what's improving, what's getting worse."

"Do you see a therapist?"

He shook his head. "Do you think I should?"

"Well, you were saying you wanted to kill yourself earlier today. That's why I'm here. Maybe your schizophrenia isn't the only aspect of your mental health that needs to be looked after."

"Maybe." He stared at the foil-blocked window, sipped his coffee.

"How often do you have people over?"

"Almost never. People stop by to ask about my sculptures sometimes. Either to buy them or take them down."

"How often do you socialize?"

"I don't have any friends, if that's what you're trying to ask. I don't work. I live off disability. All the people I knew from school have moved on with their lives. And my neighbors avoid eye contact. I'm hard to talk to. I make people uncomfortable."

"Is that why you wanted to kill yourself?"

"It's not obvious?"

"It's part of the protocol. I need to hear it in your own words."

He chuckled. "I wanted to kill myself because this is my life. I wake up around two in the afternoon. The first thing I do is piss and smoke a cigarette. If I'm hungry, I'll eat some cereal. If it's the first Thursday of the month, I'll go to the bank to deposit my disability check. When I get back, I'll fix some coffee, put on some music, and try to paint or make something. Usually I work until around midnight. Then I microwave some frozen food, take a shower, and watch some TV before bed. If it's a good night, I'll fall asleep around four a.m. If it's a bad night, I'll hear something or I'll see something and I'll get all panicky. Then I'll spend a few hours going down whatever rabbit hole my dumb head leads me to. I'll finally crash off of this adrenaline high around eight a.m., and I'll go to bed and do it all over again tomorrow. And this morning I realized that I've been doing this shit for two years, and one day I'm gonna wake up and I'll be fifty, and nothing will have changed. That's why."

"But why today?"

"What do you mean?"

"What made you call? What was different about today?"

He lit another cigarette. "Just the idea of it was different, I guess. Like the thought of killing myself had always been there, lingering, some far-off thing way down the line. But today I woke up and there it was. Right there in front of me. It was something I had to do, a chore, like taking out the trash or doing the dishes. And it made me feel really calm and peaceful in a way I couldn't remember ever feeling before. And that scared the hell out of me." He sipped his coffee. He was shaking.

I made a few summarizing notes of what he'd told me.

"What will you do if I leave here and you're left alone?"

"Don't leave me alone. It's been so nice talking to you. Don't leave me alone."

"Why? What're you going to do?"

"I don't know. Just don't leave me alone with myself."

"If you want, I can drive you to Will Durant and have you admitted. Would you like to do that?"

He stared at me, smiling, shaking his head, "You're a nice person, you know. Pretending I have a choice at this point." He put out his smoke. "Let me grab a bag, then we'll go." He walked out of the kitchen and down the hall.

I finished my coffee. By then it was cold, but with its thickness it went down easy. He really had fixed it extraordinarily strong. I'd only had one little cup, but my hands were trembling as I tucked my notebook and clipboard into my bag, slung it over my shoulder.

Wanting to keep an eye on him, I followed suit down the hallway and watched him pack. His room was pretty clean, clothes and appliances put away neatly, but the wall was cluttered with pieces of paper. From the doorway I examined them. Most were simple black-and-white sketches, more peaceful than the other ones in the house.

I studied one that portrayed a young woman riding a bike. She was leaned back, no hands, coasting, and from the way the trees and bushes were painted one got the impression that it was very windy. Then I spotted something written on the wall behind it: letters half-hidden behind artwork, and I squinted to read them. Then everything went quiet, and my ears rang, and a cold wave washed over me.

Without thinking I drifted over to it, asked, "What's this?"

"Oh, that." Brian sat down his bag, walked over, crossed his arms. "There's this girl who rides by my house all the time. I don't know where she lives or what her name is, but I always notice when she rides by. I know that's a little weird, but she's just one of those people you remember, you know?"

"No, not that," I whispered, tenderly brushing aside the painting. "That."

The penmanship was scrawled, sloppy. But the words were so familiar that I could not fail to recognize them:

"...even Asylum takes of the world for being,
Even Asylum goes mad with winter, summer, autumn and spring..."

"Oh that." He paused. "It's weird, isn't it? Confused the hell out of me when I first heard it. One of my voices used to recite it to me. Still does sometimes. Actually, he seems to be saying it more and more lately. It took me forever to figure out where it was from. Couldn't even find it with Google. One of my old professors figured it out after I asked her. It was written by this guy Garcon Orloneo. Really obscure writer. He wrote two novels and a couple books of poetry, but still I can't hardly find anything on the guy. All his books are out print, and he died a while ago. Died young, too. Mid-fifties. They say he was an alcoholic."

"What did you say his name was?"

"Garcon Orloneo."

"And when did he die?"

"Sometime in the '70s, I think."

There was a familiarity in that name I couldn't place, and the simple sound of it began an odd sort of fear in me. There was the obvious shock at the anomaly of two of my patients knowing the same endangered poem. But there was something else. And it wasn't like any fear I'd ever felt. It was a malignant fear, perambulating into each part of me. Something that had always been there, lying dormant, as if it waited years for this moment.

"What's wrong?" He asked, his voice bringing me back. "Have you heard of him?"

"No. We should get going. Are you ready?"

"Yeah."

He picked up his bag, led me out of the house. The statues appeared differently from the front porch. They were the house's own little army, standing guard. While he locked the door, I asked, "Do you know anyone named Heather Doughtery?"

"I do not. Why?"

"She's an artist too."

"Oh really, is she a sculptor?"

"I'm not sure."

He finished locking the door, dropped his key into his pocket, and walked before me through the statues. I walked slowly to my car. Their rough, painful demeanor didn't disturb me the way it had earlier. In an odd way they were almost comforting. Because I knew then that they were not evil or depraved or decomposing. They were sick. They were trying.

Why the name Garcon Orloneo was familiar to me occupied my thoughts over the next week until I remembered. It didn't come all at once, but slowly, by bit and piece, formulating into coherency.

It happened in the morning. I woke with my usual jolt just before three a.m., sweating and out of breath. As quietly as I could, I slipped out of bed and into the kitchen, poured myself a glass of water, drank it all in one go, and took my regular place before the sliding-glass door.

And it was right there, right there with my feet planted on the cold kitchen tiles that I saw it: a figure standing in our backyard, not moving, just out of reach from moonlight.

For a moment I couldn't think to move. The sight of it held me in place. Nothing about its face or body was discernable, but I knew our eyes were locked. And I began to understand, even if I hadn't known it at first.

Our dog barking loosened me from my trance, and I grabbed the biggest kitchen knife we had and flipped on the back porch lights and stepped outside. Our dog, Hank, half dachshund, half terrier, was still barking when I came out, poking his head out from the plush, oversize crate where he slept, and he only quit when I stepped onto the lawn.

The figure was gone. Hank sniffed the grass where it'd stood, huffing and growling, his tail taut in the air as he circled. My breath was fogging, and my feet were itchy and wet and cold in the nighttime grass.

Hank sounded like he'd seen it, and I had definitely seen it; but the backyard was as bare and empty as ever. The only thing in it was our daughter's prematurely bought playhouse and the tool shed.

When I felt safe enough to think it was gone, my shoulders dropped a little, releasing tension. I let the dog inside and shut off the porch light and returned the knife to its block and found myself trembling. Over the sink I splashed water on my face, and, as I lingered over it, I caught my reflection in the window.

The mirror in the bathroom confirmed what the window had

suggested: I was shrinking. Not by the inch, by the pound. My skin concaved against my bones: cheeks sunken and eyes buried. I removed the big T-shirt I slept in, studied myself. When had I lost all this weight? My ribs were visible up to my armpit, pressed so tightly to the skin that they almost broke through.

As I examined myself, a nasal cry reached me from Elaine's room. I put my shirt back on, switched off the light and walked down the hall and removed Elaine from her crib. Then I returned to the sliding-glass door.

For a while I rocked her gently, but she didn't seem to want to calm down. So I went to feed her the way I usually do. She took hold and suckled for a while and then let go and began to cry again. So I tried the other one, and the cycle repeated: She wasn't getting anything.

I returned her momentarily to her crib and searched and fumbled through our foyer closet until I found some formula. In the store I had teased Marshall for buying it, telling him it would be months before we needed it, maybe a year. But he insisted, wanted us to have everything we could possibly need when Elaine came. He was so excited to have a kid.

I prepared the powder into a cup of milk, transferred it into a bottle and tried again to feed her. At first she spat it out, shook her head. But I persisted, and after a while she'd had enough to fall back asleep.

I returned her to the crib, and cooked myself two eggs, over-easy. Though I kept trying, I couldn't remember having eaten anything the day before. It's always been my habit to skip breakfast, and I'm working when Marshall eats dinner. How someone could forget to eat was beyond me, but apparently I'd been doing it.

It had been at least a day since I'd ate, yet I wasn't hungry at all. In fact, as I ate those two eggs, even after I'd flavored them with salt and pepper and tabasco, I found myself fighting the urge to gag when it came time to swallow. Eggs have always been a favorite food of mine. "Eat enough eggs and you can run through a wall," my dad used to say. But I couldn't hardly eat half of those two tiny eggs and ended up throwing out most of it.

Then I returned to my usual spot. It was just before five a.m., another hour or so of darkness. I wanted to use all of it. My eyes found the place he'd been standing and fixed onto it until everything but the poem faded from my mind, and I caught myself repeating it in a slow, steady rhythm:

> "...even *Asylum takes of the world for being,*
> *Even Asylum goes mad with winter, summer, autumn, and spring...*"

I stayed like this until dawn. And then I knew how I knew the name Garcon Orloneo. But it was no epiphany. I'd always known it, just couldn't grasp it.

And once I realized that I knew, I raced downstairs, rummaging through everything I'd kept from school, and then there they were: the documents from my internship.

In the months between obtaining my Bachelor's and starting graduate school, I spent a summer as an intern at the biggest psychiatric hospital in the state. Very prestigious. Some of the country's most well-respected psychologists work there, and it's home to those the state has deemed criminally insane.

The tradition there, to "break in" the interns, consists of

acquainting them with some of the facility's most disturbed patients. Interns dish out medication, assist in group and individual therapy and address concerns of patients who were diagnosably antisocial.

One of these patients was Garcon Orloneo. He'd been admitted some years earlier for the murder of two young girls and was suspected of many more.

Most psychopaths (those with antisocial personality disorder is the correct terminology) are charming. They put on a harmless, amiable facade in order to get what they want, which is, in the cases of the criminally insane, their freedom, which they try to obtain by convincing psychologists of their sincerity, of their ability and desire to change: their ultimate recovery. They're masters of glib. Even veteran psychologists find it difficult not to fall for the lies of the intelligent psychopath.

But Garcon was different. He was open and honest about the enjoyment he took in his crimes, even more so about his conviction that it was the world, not him, that needed to be rehabilitated. His crimes, he believed, were simply a game he played, a game with a divine beauty that can't be understood by regular people.

Perhaps even more noticeable than his psychopathy was his narcissism. His stay at the hospital, he believed, was only a brief stop on an eternity of playing, and he had the means to leave this confinement whenever he chose. And the way he said all this was very odd, too. He had an almost poetic way of speaking, and he possessed a strange sort of intelligence.

He wouldn't say something overtly threatening or malicious. Instead, I came to believe over the months I worked there, he dropped hints, referencing something you thought or saw, something only you could know, in the middle of a conversation in such an indirect, casual way that no one but yourself could possibly notice.

I searched through every folder, every scrap of paper. Then I found it. A piece of notebook paper torn in half, reading:

"...even Asylum takes of the world for being,
Even Asylum goes mad with winter, summer, autumn and spring...

At the bottom it was signed:
"To the Dearest,
Orlo."

All my fears were vindicated, and they didn't affect me like before. Now my fear had a face and a name. It was no longer just the unknown.

I tucked the piece of paper into my pocket and went upstairs. The sun was up, and so was Marshall, eating his morning oatmeal, about to leave for work. I snuck up behind him, placed a peck on his cheek.

"There you are. Wake up early again?"

"Yeah. Feeding Elaine."

"How long have you been up?"

I shrugged. "Maybe forty-five minutes."

"You should go back to bed. It seems like you're never in bed when I wake up lately. And you go to bed so much later than I do."

"Don't worry." I smiled. "I've been taking multivitamins and fish oil. I'm gonna live to be 120."

"You better." He wiped his mouth, dropped his bowl in the sink. "Seriously though, are you feeling all right?"

The seriousness of his tone surprised me. It was valid question, but I answered it like a stupid one.

"I'm fine, Marshall. I can take care of myself. I'm a big girl."

"All right, well, I guess I should be going to work."

He pulled me in by the waist and kissed me, and I told him goodbye and then he left.

When I was sure he was gone, I looked up the number for one of the doctors I'd worked under at the psychiatric hospital. His phone rang twice before he answered. It took him a moment to remember me, but once he did, he spoke to me as an old friend. We updated each other on what we'd been up to, and then I asked about Garcon Orloneo, told him I had reason to believe he might be related to a death. He was pleased to help. He had me spell the name and promised to call back that evening with what he found.

It was about eight a.m. when we finished speaking, and I put away all my documents and cooked myself breakfast: four eggs, four pieces of toast, hash browns, sausage and orange juice. I was hungry again, hungry like I hadn't had a good meal in years.

Once finished, with my stomach full, feeling heavy and lethargic, I took a nap. My sleep was deep and dreamless, and I woke up very peacefully to Elaine's babbling down the hall. By then it was nearly eleven. So I fed her, dressed her and took her to daycare. Then I went to work.

I had my own office at William Durant, though I spent little time there. Always out on calls. But it was a slow day. So I put on some music, filled out some paperwork, waiting for a call to come in. But none did. When I was all done and tried to read a book, a real doorstopper I'd been lugging through for some time, I found that my hands were trembling, though I hadn't had any coffee.

After a while, because that poem was still bouncing around my head, and I knew no one would say anything if I left, I decided to pay Brian a visit, do a little investigating.

His place was a good drive from the hospital, and it was nearly four when I arrived. A little over a week had passed since he was admitted, so if all had gone well, he should've been home.

From the street nothing appeared different. The lawn was still bare; the statues still haunted over it. I weaved my way through them to the door. It was sealed off with yellow tape.

I paused for a moment, then knocked. I knocked and knocked. No one answered. So I slapped it with my palm, then my fist, and then I was just pounding on it, yelling his name. It felt like I had sand in my arms, and the only way to shake it loose was to hit something.

I don't know how long I did this. Perhaps I never would've stopped unless that lady had grabbed me from behind, saying, over and over again: "Calm down. Just calm down, sweetie."

I only realized I was crying when she pulled me away, felt the wind cool the streams over my cheeks. I turned to her. She had thin gray hair, thick bifocals and wore a dark green jog suit. I latched onto her.

"Do you know where Brian is?"

"Is Brian the one who lives here?"

"Yes. He lives here. I've been inside. I know him. Do you

know where he is?"

She paused, and her voice was softer when it came back. "He killed himself a few days ago."

I don't think I was particularly surprised by that. Not even sad, really; just frustrated. Brian knew more about Garcon Orloneo than I ever could, that was clear to me. And now he was gone, and all he knew he took with him.

To the lady I nodded, tried to feign some sort of grief, crossed my arms and turned around slowly. She was starting to say something when I did it. I don't know where I found the strength for it, but when I raised my leg and foot and lurched forward, the door splintered instantly around the knob.

She screamed and cursed behind me. But I didn't care about that. What I cared about were the four lines written all over the inside of Brian's home, written on the bare surfaces of every wall and table, written in the potent, yellow-brown scrawl of dried blood:

"...even Asylum takes of the world for being,
Even Asylum goes mad with winter, summer, autumn and spring...

I drove home after that. Marshall was making dinner for himself when I stormed in. I'm pretty sure I was still crying. I must've been, because he wouldn't leave me alone after he saw me. His questions interrupted his other questions, and he was just pouring out with concern. Looking back, I feel a little bad about it. But, then again, it's never been like either one of us to overreact. What did he expect?

So I ignored him, picked up the phone, went into the other

room. I dialed the same number I did that morning, and the same man answered, and we exchanged the same pleasantries. Then I asked, "So what'd you find out about Garcon Orloneo?"

"Yeah, about that. I took a look for this Garcon Orloneo guy you were telling me about. His last name is spelled O-r-l-o-n-e-o, right? Well, there's no record of him."

"Did you check under a different first name? It's French. It might have weird spelling."

"The database we use only searches by last name. There's no record by anyone of the name of Orloneo. I even asked some of the other doctors and nurses around here, see if they remembered anyone like that. They didn't. He wasn't in this hospital."

"Are you sure?"

"Almost entirely."

"Well...that's wrong. There has to be some sort of mistake. I have documentation on him."

"What sort of documentation?"

I pulled the scrap of paper on which the poem was written out of my pocket. "I have a note he left me," I managed. It had been a great effort to say that. My thoughts didn't want to become words.

"You might be mistaken. No one named Garcon Orloneo has ever been a patient at this hospital."

"No. No!" I raised my voice, then caught myself and continued, quieter. "I know he was there. I remember him very clearly. Maybe there's a glitch. His records must have been lost or something."

"I'm telling you a fact: he was never a patient here."

I went back and forth with him in the same fashion until I

SKRYPTOR

was screaming, telling him over and over that he was mistaken. But I didn't realize it until Marshall placed his hands on my shoulders, like I woke up. I heard my daughter crying in the other room. I hung up, turned around.

"What's going on with you?"

In a frenzy, through panic and sobbing, I tried to explain everything: what had happened to Heather, what Brian had told me, what I had seen earlier today, and the poem connecting them all. I wanted so badly for him to believe me. But, as I said more and more, he only seemed to get further away, and he couldn't understand me from such a distance. Finally, as if to convince him completely, I showed him the poem Orloneo had written to me.

He held it close to his face, then said: "But this is your handwriting."

"What?" I shook my head, smiled. "Don't be ridiculous."

He walked over to the fridge, peeled off my to-do list. "Look."

He held the two side by side. They had the same cursive loops, the same tight spaces in between. I tried to hold them myself, but, when my hands rose to take them, I trembled so badly that I knocked them onto the floor.

I backed away. My trembling was audible as I exhaled. When I managed to close my fists, plant my arms to my sides, I saw that Marshall was backing away. It's like we'd become a thousand miles away from each other in a fraction of a second.

"No." My words shook. "Not you."

"Olivia, just sit down for a while. Eat some dinner."

The word "eat" brought images of greasy food getting cut and chewed and mushed around and swallowed. It made me nauseous. I rushed out the front door, made it to the grass, and heaved and heaved. I wiped my mouth, stood, walked to the end of our drive.

Marshall was yelling something toward me, making his cautious way. But I wasn't listening to him; I wasn't watching for any neighbors who might look twice at a bony, tired-eyed woman with vomit caked on her shirt; and I wasn't concerned with standing right in the middle of the road beneath the moonlight as cars jumped onto the sidewalk to get around me.

No. I didn't take in any of that. My eyes were fixed on a black figure way in the distance, hidden in shadow, just beyond the reach of light. And my ears were searching beneath the shouts of my husband, beneath the cars honking at me on the road, for that laughing that would never stop.

Someone grabbed me. I tried to fight him off, but then more came, and there were people all around. They caused so much noise and commotion that it was difficult to discern anything.

Then I heard it. I didn't know how to hear it before because I have always heard it. Even then it was hardly distinguishable from the wind. So I quit listening, clutched the hands restraining me, and fell into a deep, hysterical laughter.

It's been years since we moved away from the city, settled into a little house a few miles outside a little town. Marshall thought it would be easier on me here. I tell him it is. I've always enjoyed the country.

I still search for Garcon Orloneo, and I still wake up very

early and stare out across my backyard. It's been years since my daughter's crying woke me up in the night. She has teeth now. She trots around the house on her own. But still I do it. I wake up long before anyone and stand there without moving until morning. Some nights I do not sleep at all.

I haven't found Garcon, but I see him sometimes, out there in the backyard, always hidden in shadow, always just beyond the grasp of moonlight. I think about that poem he wrote. To this day I don't know what it means. But I think I'm beginning to understand. And I write it down all over the place so I don't forget it.

I'm never hungry anymore. The weeks and the months go by, and I become smaller and smaller until there is hardly anything left of me. And the more I shrink, the more I begin to understand. I think I almost know the things that Heather was trying to say as her organs shut down. They are the same things Brian knew as he painted the walls of his home with their truth. I don't know what it is yet, but I have given so much of myself to learning it that it seems I have no choice but to continue, even if knowing it disables me from saying anything at all.

ALSO Available from Aqualamb Artists

☐ **DESCENDER by Descender** (ALR 001)
6 song debut EP. Available formats: Digipak CD, digital / streaming
90's Influenced post-hardcore. RIYL: Snapcase, Helmet, Quicksand
"Angularly aggressive hardcore that takes an abrasive shape on purpose." – CMJ

☐ **AND SO WE MARCHED by Descender** (ALR 002)
4 song EP. Available formats: Printed book, digital / streaming
90's Influenced post-hardcore. RIYL: Snapcase, Helmet, Quicksand
"...a 21st Century compliant post-hardcore band that was raised on metal and got dosed with a tab of AmRep..."– Jaded Scenster

☐ **TAKING DRUGS TO MAKE MUSIC TO SELL CARS TO**
by Human Highlight Reel (ALR 003)
4 song debut EP. Available formats: Vinyl record, printed book, digital / streaming
Instrumental post-rock. RIYL: Maserati, June of 44, Russian Circles
"Aces instrumental post rock. Think Russian Circles or perhaps a more metal Seam..." – Jaded Scenster

☐ **JUDGE by Vagina Panther** (ALR 004)
5 song EP. Available formats: Printed book, digital / streaming
Heavy female-fronted garage rock. RIYL: QOTSA, Cheeseburger, Fu Manchu, Stooges
"Vagina Panther rocks." – Billboard

☐ **BLACK BLACK BLACK by Black Black Black** (ALR 005)
12 song debut LP. Available formats: Vinyl record, printed book, digital / streaming
Melodic death rock. RIYL: Akimbo, Torche, Lungfish, Black Flag
"Brooklyn-by-way-of-Ohio doomsters offer up a big, nasty salute to gas tanks and goat hooves. It all coalesces to form one ravaging feast of melodic death rock that will satiate all your salacious needs, be it Nether-deity worshiping or rock star living." – Broken Beard

☐ **GODMAKER by Godmaker** (ALR 007)
4 song debut LP. Available formats: Vinyl record, printed book, digital / streaming
Doomy sludge metal. RIYL: High on Fire, Red Fang, Mastodon, The Sword
"An example of genuine out of-nowhere brilliance. A patient drawn out campaign of aggression." – Relix

☐ **THE SPACE MERCHANTS by The Space Merchants** (ALR 008)
8 song debut LP. Available formats: Printed book, digital / streaming
Whiskey-soaked space-rock. RIYL: Black Mountain, Dead Meadow, The Besnard Lakes
"A unique brand of lo-fi psych rock... their huge-yet-minimal sound, mixing psych with blues and country style riffs to make something great." – Magnet

☐ **HIRAM-MAXIM by Hiram-Maxim** (ALR 009)
4 song debut LP. Available formats: Vinyl record, printed book, digital / streaming
Noisy experimental doomgaze. RIYL: Swans, Suicide, Pink Floyd, Oxbow
"Builds into an apocalyptic fervor before dissipating into a cloudy haze & ending before you've had your fill." – VICE

☐ **ALTERED STATES OF DEATH AND GRACE by Black Black Black** (ALR 010)
10 song sophomore LP. Available formats: Vinyl record, printed book, digital / streaming
Melodic death rock. RIYL: Akimbo, Torche, Lungfish, Black Flag
"...the kind of good-natured misanthropy of bands like Whores or KEN mode, but the musical gestures beneath the noisy exterior are all forward-charging, Kyuss-worshipping sludge n' roll. It's basically underground metal's version of a radio banger." – BrooklynVegan

☐ **TRESPASSES by Nathaniel Shannon & The Vanishing Twin** (ALR 011)
15 song debut LP. Available formats: Printed book, digital / streaming
Unsettling bedroom recording darkness. RIYL: Lanegan, Badalemnti, Springsteen, Waits
"An unsettling yet captivating collection of songs compiled from a decade of bedroom recordings... Shannon's spoken word-style vocals over haunting and minimalist instrumentals lend a creepy atmosphere to the record." – Decibel

☐ **FERA by Husbandry** (ALR 012)
8 song debut LP. Available formats: Printed book, CD, digital / streaming
Female-fronted math rock meets post-hardcore. RIYL: Mars Volta, Glassjaw, Refused, Deftones
"It's hard to believe that Husbandry is not the biggest band in the world. They're heavy and mathy, chaos wrapped in hard rock and heavy metal." – Nerdist

☐ **MURDEREDMAN by MURDEREDMAN** (ALR 013)
8 song sophomore LP. Available formats: Vinyl record, printed book, digital / streaming
Post-punk inspired noise rock. RIYL: Savages, Bauhaus, Boris, Killing Joke
"A patient and disciplined examination of anxiety and melancholy underpinned with a cathartic tension-and-release structure that borrows from goth, post-metal, and no-wave..." – New Noise Magazine

☐ **IN TENSIONS by Lo-Pan** (ALR 014)
5 song EP. Available formats: Vinyl record, printed book, CD, digital / streaming
Anthemic desert rock. RIYL: Soundgarden, ASG, Torche, Red Fang
"Calling Lo-Pan a stoner band is a disservice to the amalgam of influences the band successfully merges together: the soulful alt rock of the 90s with a thundering doom/sludge sound that's equal parts immediate and timeless." – Nine Circles

☐ **GHOSTS by Hiram-Maxim** (ALR 015)
7 song LP. Available formats: Vinyl record, printed book, digital / streaming
Noisy experimental doomgaze. RIYL: Swans, Suicide, Pink Floyd, Oxbow
"Everything is awash in mesmerizing ambient skree and squalls of atonal feedback. Think an extended, updated version of side 2 of Black Flag's My War." – Hellride Music

☐ **KISS THE DIRT by The Space Merchants** (ALR 016)
10 song sophomore LP. Available formats: Vinyl record, printed book, digital / streaming
Whiskey-soaked space-rock. RIYL: Black Mountain, Dead Meadow, The Besnard Lakes
"[T]he sonic equivalent of having an acid trip in the bathroom between Woodstock and a ZZ Top concert in '69" – New Noise Magazine

☐ **BAD WEEDS NEVER DIE by Husbandry** (ALR 017)
5 song EP. Available formats: Printed book, CD, digital / streaming
Female-fronted math rock meets post-hardcore. RIYL: Mars Volta, Glassjaw, Refused, Deftones
"While retaining their bold go-anywhere style, the EP is a more streamlined and focused effort, signaling a greater maturity and command of recording." – Echoes and Dust

☐ **BY THE GRACE OF BLOOD AND GUTS by Haan** (ALR 018)
8 song LP. Available formats: Printed book, Vinyl, CD, digital / streaming
Noise, Grime, Sludge, Metal, Rock. RIYL: Unsane, Melvins, Swans, Helmet, Clutch
"If Melvins and Unsane had a kid while under the influence of hallucinogens" – Metal Insider

☐ **LUMINOUS VOLUMES by Skryptor** (ALR 019)
7 song LP. Available formats: Vinyl, Printed book, CD, digital / streaming
Noise, Math rock, Prog. RIYL: craw, Dazzling Killmen, Don Cabellero
"Galloping, off-kilter and unabashedly victorious, proggy noise-rock outfit Skryptor's takes hard-rock/psychedelic throwback tropes, flips them on their heads and stretches it all into an adventurous march through endlessly shifting soundscapes."" – Revolver

☐ **DEAD INSIDE by Frayle** (ALR 021)
7 song 7". Alchemy Box: Printed book, Vinyl, CD, digital / streaming
Heavy witch doom. RIYL: Chelsea Wolfe, Portis Head, Sleep, Sunn O)))
"Trades in dark psychedelics and heavy, dripping drums that punctuate the riffing that plays in and around vocalist Gwyn Strang's superb voice." – Nine Circles

☐ **SUBTLE by Lo-Pan** (ALR 022)
11 song LP. Available formats: Vinyl, Printed book, CD, digital / streaming
Anthemic desert rock. RIYL: Soundgarden, ASG, Torche, Red Fang
Subtle was produced by James Brown (NIN, Foo Fighters, Ghost) and mastered by Ted Jensen (Mastodon, Deftones, Bad Company, GNR).

The music for *Luminous Volumes*
can be downloaded via the link below:

aqualamb.org/019